THE FIRST
ASTROWITCHES

THE FIRST ASTROWITCHES

MARIAN T. PLACE

Illustrated by Tom O'Sullivan

DODD, MEAD & COMPANY·
New York

F
P

1 2 3 4 5 6 7 8 9 10

Library of Congress Cataloging in Publication Data

Place, Marian T. (Marian Templeton), date
  The first astrowitches.

  Summary: Two young witches stow away on a space mis-
sion in an effort to contact a witches' space exploring
expedition that has not been heard from in a long time.
  1. Children's stories, American. [1. Witches—
Fiction. 2. Science fiction] I. O'Sullivan, Tom, ill.
II. Title.
PZ7.P69Fi 1984   [Fic]   84-10266
ISBN 0-396-08456-7

To Judy P. Laird

Contents

1
Bean Soup Fog

Dense fog enveloped a school bus transporting students from Myrtlewood School to cross streets nearest their homes. Only fourth through sixth graders rode the late afternoon Activity Bus which left the school-grounds at 4:15 P.M. By that time soccer, volleyball, gymnastics, and chorus activities were over for the day.

The driver asked the students to be quiet so he could concentrate on driving in the fog. They cooperated 100 percent. There was no shouting, punching, wrestling, snatching caps, or throwing books. Even the sixth grade jocks, who monopolized the back seat by the emergency door, behaved.

None were aware that one pupil on the bus was the only Junior Wizard attending an elementary school anywhere in the United States. He answered to the name of Richard Oaw, although his real name was Witchard. Two years earlier when he was ten and enrolled in the fourth grade at Myrtlewood, the school clerk thought he lisped. She wrote *Richard* on the Student Enrollment Form, instead of Witchard.

"And your last name?" she asked.

Witchard explained he did not have a last name because he was a witch. "Witches don't need last names because we're all members of the same family."

The clerk smiled. "You don't look like a witch."

His green eyes sparkled because he had been raised to play tricks on earthlings. "Honest. I really am a witch. My family belongs to the OAW."

"O A W?" she spelled out.

He nodded. "The Organization of American Witches."

The telephone jangled. Students clamored to buy milk tickets. It was almost time for the First Period bell to ring. The clerk hurriedly enrolled him as Richard Oaw who lived on Dogwood Lane and had no telephone.

Now that he was twelve, except for being a little short and having large feet, Witchard looked like any ordinary sixth grader. He was popular with his classmates and homeroom teacher, Mr. Abbott, and earned good grades. No one suspected he was a witch, or became suspicious if he slipped in a witchly trick now and then.

For example, from the moment he stepped onto the

school bus that day and raced a pal, Ted, to a seat, Witchard glared fiercely out of the window. All witches hated fog because its clammy wetness helped pollutants in the air to soak into their clothing and brooms. After too many flights in fog, their dresses and hats sprouted green furry mold, their shoe buckles tarnished, and their brooms shed bristles.

Witchard mumbled several magic words which commanded, "Fog, fog, go away. *Don't* come again another day."

"What'd you say?" Ted whispered. He was used to his pal's mumbling.

"I told the fog to get lost."

"Hah! Fat chance."

Witchard sighed. If only he had enough magic power to banish the mucky stuff. Then he remembered that neither his grandmother nor aunt could banish fog, and they were Senior Witches. He felt better.

Ted frowned. "Gee, look how dark it is already."

"So what? Don't crawl the wall. You'll be home before dark."

Witchard was glad he wasn't afraid of the dark. Until he was ten, he didn't even know there was such a thing as daylight. He was strictly a night flier, and loved swishing around on his personal broom, Splinters. Like all members of the witch family, not just in North America but worldwide, he possessed night sight as sharp as his owl friends. Thanks to limited magic powers bestowed on Junior Witches and Junior Wizards for their protection, he could see through walls and around corners.

On his tenth birthday his grandmother, called Gramwitch, changed him from a night flier to a day witch. She was forced to take this bold step to save him from withering away from loneliness. Witchard had never known other witchlings. While there were a half dozen Senior Witches assigned by the OAW to fly haunt-and-scare routes in Oregon, there were no witchlings his age living closer than two hundred miles. Only one other, a girl named Witcheena, lived anywhere near Gramwitch and her family, and Witchard only saw her at witch conventions. Then his parents had volunteered for the witches' space exploring expedition. Witchard missed them so much Gramwitch thought he would really wither away. Rather than lose her precious grandson, she let him enroll at Myrtlewood School in a hilly wooded suburb of Portland.

Gramwitch did not expect him to rely solely on magic tricks to excel in school. She programmed his brain so he could read and write at fourth grade level. She also provided contact lenses to correct the blurred vision all witches suffer when exposed to daylight, or artificial light.

After his first experience eating in the school cafeteria and riding home in a school bus, she conjured up earplugs to protect his supersensitive hearing. Neither the earplugs nor his pointed ears showed because his wiry brown hair covered both. He wore jeans, T-shirts, and Nikes to school. When he needed written permission to play soccer, she wrote a note which enabled him to ride home on the Activity Bus.

This particular day wisps of fog swirled inside the bus every time the driver braked to a stop and opened the door. The Pollution Index figure, written on the blackboard every morning, was 79: Very High. For the fourth day in a row a citywide Pollution Alert was in effect. Students were instructed to cover their mouths and noses with handkerchiefs or paper masks before leaving the bus, and not to run home.

A glance in the rearview mirror told the driver some of his passengers were very tense. "Relax, kids. Talk if you want to, but keep the volume down. Okay?"

Immediately Ted grumped, "Yuck! No bike riding in that pea soup out there."

"Bean soup," Witchard said, chortling. "Pea soup is barf green. That fog is as yellow as cafeteria bean soup."

"Right. Hey, how about coming to my house? Mom bought me a new video game."

Witchard shook his head. "I've got to go straight

home. Gram and my aunt are still awfully sick. I'll take a rain check."

Ted waggled his eyebrows. "How about a fog check?"

"Fog check? Ha ha. You're really sharp today, pal."

Witchard changed the subject to the chances their room team had to win the district sixth grade soccer championship.

Finally the driver called out, "Pinewood!"

Ted zipped his jacket and pulled the hood over his head. "See you." He covered his face with his handkerchief, clumped down the steps and disappeared into the fog.

Immediately Witchard popped his contact lenses out of his eyes. Daylight had darkened, so he didn't need them. He glared into the fog as the bus trundled on through the housing development. Ever since hearing Mr. Abbott talk about acid fog, which scientists claimed damaged the environment like acid rain, he wondered if fog could have caused his grandmother's and Aunt Scarey's recent illness. Since pollution was a Number One problem for all witches, he should at least try to discover whether today's fog was acid or not.

He mumbled the proper magic phrase which provided him with two seconds of X-ray vision. He observed nothing alarming. The fog seemed to be acid-free. It was probably full of pollutants, but other than

15

that, it was the old-fashioned kind which rolled in whenever a Pacific storm front moved across the state.

Not being able to do anything about the weather, he relaxed.

Less than a quarter hour later, the bus drove out of the housing development and onto a county road bordered with small farms and orchards. Near the end of the route the driver called, "Dogwood!"

Witchard tied his handkerchief over his face, zipped his jacket, and covered his head. "Thanks for the safe ride. G'night," he said to the driver before he stepped down onto the road.

He waited until the blinking bus lights vanished before whistling for his guard cat, Tom. The sleek black creature with orange-colored eyes streaked out from under an azalea bush, and leaped onto his master's shoulder.

Tom accompanied Witchard to school because only on rare occasions might a witchling or Junior Witch be absent from home without a guardian. When Tom trailed his master into the fourth grade classroom, the boys and girls had voted him their mascot. Tom was given complete freedom in the classroom that year, the next, and continued as mascot for his master's sixth grade homeroom. However, no animals were allowed on the bus, so Tom swooshed on his own legs to and from school.

"Hang on!" Witchard shouted.

Since he rode the bus, not his broom, he swooshed at lightning speed along a muddy lane. He skidded to a stop before a large mound of wild blackberry vines. These hid a small cottage from public view. Muttering another magic phrase and stamping his left foot caused the vines to separate for five seconds. Quickly he pushed through, opened the door, and slipped inside the cold dark kitchen of his home.

2
Witchard's World

Immediately Witchard magicked a smokeless fire to crackle merrily in the fireplace. Then he stood motionless until he heard his grandmother and aunt snoring. They sounded awful, but at least they were still breathing.

Gramwitch was to blame for their being ill. The Organization of American Witches no longer required members to fly their haunt-and-scare routes during fog, heavy rain, hurricanes, or pollution alerts. Interrupting television broadcasts, scrambling traffic, wailing from housetops, blowing smoke down chimneys, and other forms of haunting, scaring, and mischief-making now were permitted only during decent weather and on weekdays.

Witchard's grandmother and aunt could have stayed home by the fire, sipping their favorite brew, instead of flitting around in the dense fog that blanketed the area. But Gramwitch insisted it was safer then to fly about, gathering nuts, berries, herbs, snails, and other delicacies she used in making spiced gluck and other concoctions. The two came home soaking wet. The chill dampness or polluted air had brought on a severe attack of the wheezies. They dosed themselves with every cure-all known to witches. Nothing helped. They lost sleep, and had great difficulty breathing. The wheezies worsened.

Tom jumped down and led the way across the kitchen. The family lived in an abandoned walnut grower's home. It was deserted when the surrounding orchard was sold to real estate developers. Many handsome trees were bulldozed away and replaced with town houses. Only three acres remained untouched when the developers ran out of funds. Since then the little vine-covered cottage provided a snug haven for the witch family assigned to haunt-and-scare routes between Portland and the coast. OAW members provided this service for 90 percent of the counties in the United States.

Witchard trailed Tom into a hallway. They paused at the door of a bedroom crowded with Gramwitch's four-poster bed. Her pointed hat and Scarey's topped two bedposts while their pet bats clung to the remaining ones. Their elderly cats slept at the foot of the bed. Scarey snored softly, Gramwitch fitfully.

19

"Gram sounds worse," Witchard fretted. "What'll I do?"

Tom curled up and pretended to sleep.

"Let them sleep? Okay."

He walked past the room used by his parents, Dearie and Darrell, before they joined a pioneering space exploration group sponsored by the OAW. Pollution was thinning the ranks of witches at an alarming rate. A number of young and still vigorous Senior Witches like Dearie and Darrell volunteered to probe outer space, and locate a pollution-free planet where all witches could settle before their dwindling numbers withered away to zero.

The Pioneers, as they called themselves, conjured up a streamlined space bus modeled after NASA orbiters, *Challenger* and *Columbia*. It was not burdened with the tons of bulky equipment earthlings required to orbit the Earth. The Pioneers relied on magic batteries, small rocket thrusters, and merging the magic power of all on board to lift off from Earth and hurtle on to outer space.

The Pioneers' space vehicle was furnished with triple-pane thermal glass canopies on top and bottom for space viewing. There were reclining couches with seat belts to restrain the volunteers from floating and tumbling about while in a state of weightlessness.

They had promised to transmit progress reports daily from space to Earth by means of a shortwave radio set, or transceiver, on board. It would be manned by two members working twelve-hour shifts. Their duties would include transmitting messages to Earth, and standing by to receive transmissions from OAW headquarters and their families.

When not on duty, the remaining members would

21

magic themselves into a sleeplike state so they never got hungry or had to go to the bathroom. They would subsist on a single daily food-and-vitamin pill.

Their families expected to receive their messages, broadcast in witch language, on family-owned transceivers. The transmitting and receiving was carried out on WF, witch frequencies known only to witches.

Tragically, not one message had been received from the Pioneers since their departure thirty months ago. Rumor spread through witchdom that the Pioneers were lost in space, and would never return. Witchard grieved until he almost withered away. Gramwitch saved him by sending him to school. "In time," she hinted, "you might learn how to contact your parents."

Witchard believed her with all his heart.

So far he had not succeeded, but he was not discouraged. If the smartest Senior Witches and Wizards in the OAW hadn't found the answer, how could he? Still, he would keep trying.

Witchard and Tom went on into Witchard's own bedroom. There he changed into the uniform every Junior Wizard must wear at home and on night flights: dark green slacks and shirt, leather loafers with copper buckles, and a floppy-brimmed pointed hat.

Tiptoeing to the kitchen, he filled the kettle from a rain barrel placed under a hole in the roof. He hung it on a crane beside the fireplace. "Want to watch Spacevision?" he asked Tom.

"Meow!" the guard cat responded enthusiastically.

Witchard turned on the set and curled up in one of three rockers facing the fireplace. Tom settled on his lap. Ever since he was a witchling, Witchard had watched reruns of films of the Mercury and Gemini flights, the moon walks, Pioneer 10's progress, and successful shuttle orbits. He and Tom also enjoyed viewing *Star Trek*, *Battle Star Galactica*, and *Star Wars*.

He and Ted had gone to see the movie, *E.T.—The Extra-Terrestrial*, four times. He watched every move E.T. made in trying to contact the space ship which had brought him to Earth and left without him. When his message got through and he was rescued, Witchard almost broke his hands clapping. If E.T. could contact space from Earth, then so could he.

Watching space adventures helped him imagine what Dearie and Darrell might be doing, and made him feel a little less lonely. He rarely moped about their being gone, though now and then he cried himself to sleep. Because witches cry dry, he shed no tears.

Occasionally he suffered nightmares in which the Pioneers were being destroyed by solar winds or space pirates. When he started screaming, his Aunt Scarey comforted him. "Dearie and Darrell are all right," she crooned repeatedly until the nightmare vanished.

"Maybe the Pioneers couldn't fly as fast as they hoped and it is taking longer to find a nice planet. They have to map it, and take photographs, and plant our flag there before flying home. Who knows? They may be on their way home now!" Scarey kissed his cheek, and tucked the quilt under his chin. "Sweet dreams, darling."

"Love you," he murmured as he closed his eyes.

After that, during study periods at school or whenever he lay awake nights, he pondered what could be causing the problem. Something must be blocking two-way Earth-outer space voice transmissions on the WF. He should be searching for it.

A marvelous idea gripped his imagination. If he succeeded in discovering the right frequency, he would be famous! The Supreme, president of the OAW, would present him a gold medal at the national convention.

Where to start? he asked himself feverishly. He glared at the family transceiver, a combined radio transmitter and receiver. It was so old it wasn't even transistorized. Not even the wisest wizard in all OAW could locate any new WF with that old clunker.

He had waited until his grandmother was in a good mood before pestering her. "I sure wish we had a witch ham radio powerful enough to test for new frequencies."

She shook her hat. "The old one is good enough."

"Aw, it's no stronger than Ted's walkie-talkie," he remarked disgustedly. "If I had a new one, I bet I could put us in contact with Dearie and Darrell."

"Suppose you failed? What then?"

"Well, I'd do what I did lots of times playing touch football. When someone tried to block me from making a touchdown, I went around his block."

"And if that failed?"

His jaw sagged. "Gram, don't you have any faith in me?"

"Of course, but—"

Suddenly he smiled craftily. "If I solve the problem, you will have the most famous grandson in witchdom."

The old crone's objections melted faster than ice cream. "All right, I'll conjure up something. I won't have a minute's peace until I do."

Witchard gave her a hug and kiss. "Make it powerful, Gram."

"Yes, yes! Now hush while I do some heavy conjuring."

She shook her hat, and settled in her rocking chair. She programmed commands into her brain, but nothing happened. "Scarey, come closer. You, too, Witchard. Let's put our hats together. I need more power."

Joining the tips of the hats speeded input and output of information faster than earthlings using computer software discs.

Soon a new WF shortwave radio transceiver appeared. Scarey had conjured up a nice table, so it settled next to the Spacevision.

That night, and many more, Gramwitch and Scarey pulled their rockers alongside Witchard's as he dialed one WF band after another. He tuned in on all three witch frequencies, and heard witches and wizards around the nation transmitting in their native language. Yet no matter how he experimented, he never received one *dit* or *dot* of witch language from the Pioneers.

"I give up," he declared finally. "Finding a new frequency can't be the answer, or I'd have located one. Witchit!" He was disgusted with himself.

"You've been trying too hard. Rest a few nights," Scarey suggested.

Witchard dragged off to bed. He knew he was never going to locate his folks. He was never going to be famous. If only he could talk to someone his age who would understand.

But how could he? The only thing he was allowed to say at school was that his parents were away. He wouldn't dare peep about their being off in space, or his trying to contact them on the WF. If he talked about witch ham operators and witch frequencies, Mr. Abbott would send him to the school counselor.

Maybe Ted would understand. He didn't have his father at home, either.

The next afternoon while he and Ted rode home on the Activity Bus, Witchard confided, "I've given up hope of ever hearing from my folks."

Ted laid an arm across his shoulders. "That's rough. I know. I feel the same way about my Dad. Mom and I haven't heard from him since he took off. Not even on birthdays or Christmas. He left to do his own thing. Mom says when he gets tired of that, he'll come back and take me camping. There's nothing I can do to bring him back. All I can do is sit and wait, and not give up hope. If I can do it, so can you, pal. Cheer up. Promise?"

Witchard promised because he felt so much luckier than Ted. Dearie and Darrell hadn't walked out on him. He knew about where they were, and why it was taking them so long. If he wasn't receiving their messages, it was because something was blocking them.

He stopped moping, and started thinking to himself about what to try next. He couldn't sit around and wait, like Ted. He had to be doing something.

The arrival of a winter storm gave him plenty of time to sit before the fire, with Tom on his lap, and think. Gramwitch and Scarey had caught terrible colds after flying in dense fog. These worsened into severe lung congestion. Neither would eat, but kept him busy heating water and making their special brew.

Night after night Witchard nursed them, in-between sitting in his rocker and thinking, and reading material brought home from the school library. Block . . . block . . . that had to be the problem. If he was playing touch football, he would run around the

27

player blocking him. But how could he run around an unknown, unseen interference?

The next night he expected to ask Gram to conjure up more power for the new transceiver. He wanted to try bouncing signals to the moon, and find out if he could receive them. But Gram could hardly breathe. She had no strength for conjuring, nor did Scarey.

He began thinking about the *Challenger* and *Columbia*. Nothing blocked their lift-off, or orbiting, or conversations with Ground Control at Houston. People all over the world tuned in on them. Too bad he couldn't rocket into space on his own, and transmit from there to the Pioneers.

The idea was so outlandish he laughed until his ribs ached. But the notion stuck like glue to his brain. It dangled dazzling possibilities.

He snapped his fingers. He'd explore that idea after Gram and Scarey recovered. He went to bed happy.

The next afternoon he sat in his rocker, watching Spacevision and waiting for the two to call for hot brew.

3

Witchard Prepares Goop

Before long Gramwitch called out, "W-i-tchard!"

When he rushed to her side she croaked, "Help me to my rocking chair. I can't stand to stay in bed one more minute. But you'll have to help me. I'm too weak to walk alone."

"Me, too," Scarey whispered.

Although alarmed, he greeted both cheerily. "You'll feel better sitting close to the fire. I put the kettle on so you wouldn't have to wait for a hot drink."

Both had gone to bed without changing from their black dresses into purple flannel nightgowns and nightcaps. Witchard slipped Gram's shoes on her bony feet, raised her to a sitting position and slid her feet onto the floor. With her leaning on him and Tom dragging her hat and shawl, he moved her to her rocking chair by the fireplace. Like all witches, she and Scarey preferred rocking chairs to straight chairs because the rocking motions recharged their magic power.

"Hang on while I fix your shawl." He laid it around her shoulders, then crossed the ends over her chest and tied them to the arm rests. That kept her from falling out on her long nose. "I'll fix your brew as soon as I help Scarey."

Since his aunt was as thin as a feather, he had no trouble guiding her to her rocking chair.

"Thank you, dear boy," she said between wheezes.

He patted her cheek. "Hot spiced brew coming up fast."

He opened the tin of powdered brew mix made from herbs, dried lightning bugs, powdered thunder eggs, and other delicacies. During the five o'clock family hour every night, the three witches always drank a mug or two. Witchard was shocked to find barely enough mix for two servings. "Witchit! What will I do if they want more? I better drink plain hot water."

A glance into other tins revealed there was nothing to prepare for supper—no spiced gluck, crawdad stew makings, or mushroom dumpling dough. It was just as well. Gramwitch had never programmed him to cook. She was queen of the kitchen, and didn't like anyone, even her daughter, messing around. As he poured hot water on the last of the brew powder, a hundred ideas raced around in his brain. Somehow he had to put together a tempting meal. Gram and Scarey had not eaten a nourishing meal in days.

As the old and young crones sipped their brew, they kept him hopping.

"I'm freezing! Fetch me another shawl."

"Command more heat. Wet a cloth to lay on my throbbing head."

He couldn't seem to do anything to satisfy his grandmother. But Scarey told him, "Darling, without your tender loving care we might wither away."

Hinting they might be on the verge of withering away to dust frightened him. He couldn't bear to think of being alone until his parents returned. His outer shell of cheerfulness crumpled. He faced the fact that the two crones did show signs of withering. He must do something, and quickly!

"We're out of food and brew mix," he announced. "You're too weak to conjure up anything. Let me swoosh to the supermarket for groceries. I'll need some money."

That Gramwitch did not argue told him how very ill she was. She waggled a finger at the can where she banked her money. It sailed through the air onto her lap.

"Can I leave Tom? Cats are not allowed in stores."

Gramwitch shook her hat. "Yes. Hurry. I'm hungry."

Witchard tied a handkerchief over his face, slipped on his yellow slicker, and commanded the vines to part. He didn't try to fly because Splinters could not carry him and groceries, too. Instead he swooshed speedily to the supermarket three miles away. Before entering he lowered his handkerchief so the clerks would not mistake him for a bandit. Then he grabbed a cart and hurried to the Health Foods section where he had shopped before with Ted.

Recalling from his memory something learned in a study unit on nutrition, he placed eggs, yeast powder, wheat germ, canned milk, apricot nectar, and bananas in the cart. On the way to the check-out stand he remembered peanut butter and jelly sandwiches were good. The makings went into the cart.

"Witchit! I forgot stuff for brew mix."

He recalled class discussion on the perils of too much caffeine, and the stimulants in coffee, cocoa, and sugar. But his family needed pepping up! He tossed small containers of powered coffee, cocoa, and sugar cubes in the basket. Then he hurried to the check-out stand.

"Please use a double bag," he asked the checker politely. "I have to carry everything home."

The cashier obliged, rang up the items and handed him his change. "Have a nice evening."

"Don't I wish!" he grumbled, rushing out the door.

Since the groceries were heavy, he did not make as

fast time on the return trip. The moment he stepped inside, Gramwitch fretted, "What took you so long? I want more brew this minute."

Witchard gritted his teeth. "Yes, ma'am."

This time he lined up three mugs because he was ravenous. Into each he placed a spoonful of instant coffee, one of cocoa, and two sugar cubes. After stirring in boiling water, he handed one mug to Gram and another to Scarey. "Try this. I made it from things I learned about at school."

Scarey took a sip. "Why, it's delicious. What did you use?"

Gram slurped noisily. "Argh! What's this? Why didn't you use my brew mix?"

"It's all gone," he shouted so she would be certain to hear.

The more she slurped, the better she liked it. "Not bad for a Junior Wizard," she remarked to her daughter.

Scarey agreed. "I'm feeling better already."

Witchard cautioned them not to drink too fast. "That stuff will blow your hats off."

The witches chortled wheezily.

Witchard dusted off the blender Scarey had conjured up after seeing one advertised on Spacevision. It did not require batteries or an electrical plug-in. He punched holes in the cans of milk and nectar, and poured some of each into the blender's glass container. Then he added other ingredients, including two peeled bananas. Every time he stopped the blender's brief surges of whirring, he sampled the contents.

"Super-power goop ready to slurp," he called cheerfully. He filled each mug half full of the thick creamy concoction.

34

Gramwitch fussed. "It's too thick to drink. Hand me a spoon."

Scarey stuck a finger in her mug and licked it clean. "This is scrumptious."

Witchard handed each a spoon. "You haven't eaten for days. Take it easy or you'll have upset stomachs. I'll turn on the Spacevision. When the evening news broadcast is over, I'll serve more goop. Okay?"

Both bobbed their hats.

Meantime Tom and the two elderly cats had leaped onto the cupboard and were lapping the creamy drink. Witchard shooed them off, filled a saucer and placed it on the floor for them. At last he could sprawl in his rocker and enjoy his goop.

As he watched Gram and Scarey, he hoped drinking his goop restored their health. His next job should be convincing his grandmother to shop at the supermarket during the stormy fall and winter weather. He wasn't certain that flying in the rain and polluted fog had made them ill, but getting soaked and chilled surely brought on the attack of the wheezies. Another attack might put them down. Somehow he had to talk Gram into changing her recipes so she could use packaged foods for a few months.

He noticed that the first segment of the evening news had concluded. The usual parade of commercials flashed on the screen. He started to get up to serve more goop when a new commercial came on. It featured a sweet old lady coughing horrendously. Her worried family offered her cough syrup and cold capsules.

She pushed them away. "No, no! I must have clean air, or I shall die! Clean the air! Oh, please, clean the air!"

Her family wrung their hands in despair. They did not know how to clean the air.

In a flash a curly-wigged fairy flew into the bedroom and placed a box on the bedside table. The fairy tapped the box with her wand. Presto! Waves of lemon-scented charcoal-filtered air gushed from the box. The dear old lady breathed deeply. In two seconds she stopped coughing. "I can breathe again! I can breathe, thanks to lemon-scented Freshair."

An announcer, costumed in a doctor's smock, walked in and explained the wonders of the Freshair machine. It could be purchased at local stores, and produced 99 percent pollution-free air.

Witchard leaped to his feet. "Gram! That's what you and Scarey need. Conjure up one and you'll cure your wheezies."

"I can't," she croaked. "I don't have enough strength, and neither does Scarey."

"Then give me some more money, and I'll swoosh back to the supermarket and buy one right now."

Gram didn't argue. Again Witchard covered his face,

donned his slicker, parted the vines and swooshed off into the chill fog. In twenty minutes he returned with a carton. He lifted the Freshair machine from it, and placed it on top of the Spacevision. Scarey magicked it so it would work without batteries or electricity.

As the machine sucked the musty, dusty kitchen air through the charcoal filter and blew it out again, the room was filled with lemon-scented filtered air. Everyone, including the cats, inhaled and exhaled vigorously. For an hour all breathed the fresher air, sipped goop, and rocked. The witches' wheezies did not disappear as readily as happened during the commerical. However, in thirty minutes Gramwitch felt 1000 percent better.

She complimented her grandson. "Thanks to your brew and goop, and the Freshair machine, neither Scarey nor I will wither away."

Witchard whooped for joy. "Let's run the machine all night. I'll stay awake and serve you goop every hour."

Scarey offered, "You rest in-between serving us. I'll wake you every hour."

Gram managed a smile. "Off to bed, young wizard."

By morning Scarey was strong enough to walk unaided to her bed. Gramwitch sounded stronger. Witchard made another batch of goop, rinsed the mugs, and placed everything on a table at Scarey's side of the bed. He placed the Freshair machine at the foot.

Scarey laid her hand against his cheek. "We'll be fine. Have a good day at school."

Gramwitch was snoring already, so he whispered, "Did I discover a cure for the wheezies? Would The Supreme award me a gold medal for what I did?"

His aunt shook her head. "Sorry, darling. Witches have practiced medicine for centuries." She patted his hand. "Don't worry. You'll earn a gold medal some day."

Witchard tucked the quilt under her chin. He could always count on his aunt to make him feel good. Who wouldn't earn a gold medal some day with encouragement like that?

4

The Christmas Program

Within a few days the family routine was almost back to normal. Gram wanted to resume preparing the family meals, only the cupboard was bare. Although the weather had cleared, it was too cold for her to venture out. When Witchard returned from school, she handed him some money. "You'll have to go to the store."

Witchard swooshed over in the dark. He couldn't wait to surprise her by bringing home fresh fruits and vegetables, as well as goop ingredients. When he stepped back into the kitchen, he announced, "Have I got a surprise for you!"

Scarey clapped her hands. "I'll set the table."

She mumbled magic words, stamped both feet, and hopped aside. A fully-set table appeared, complete with straight chairs, cobweb napkins, and glowing candles.

Witchard made a fearful racket in the kitchen, but soon called, "Take your places."

The menu included still-warm store-barbecued chicken, steaming chili, and a salad of lettuce, avocado, orange slices, raw zucchini, and unsalted nuts. He served with a flourish and filled the mugs with blackberry tea.

Both Senior Witches ate with gusto, smacking their lips and slurping the tea. Then they asked for seconds.

He hadn't planned on second helpings. "Better not. You'll gain weight. The brooms will buck you off."

Scarey agreed. "Let's watch Spacevision instead."

Witchard decided the proper time had arrived to present his new plan. "When it's cold and rainy, why don't you two shop at the supermarket? Other witches do in the Midwest and New England. We've heard them talking about it on the WF. Wait until spring to hunt for your favorite bulbs and snails."

Gram burped. "I suppose it wouldn't hurt. That salad was superb."

"It would be nice," Scarey exclaimed. "We would avoid another attack of the wheezies, wouldn't we? We'd have to change into senior citizen clothes, but I'd enjoy wearing something pretty for a change."

Witchard decided he dared make another suggestion. "Another way to avoid getting sick again is for you both to wear slickers. I sure like the yellow one I wear to school. There's no rule against wearing slickers to match your black dresses. One of our lady teachers wears a black silky-looking one that is just beautiful."

Gramwitch moved to her rocker while Scarey cleared the table and tidied the kitchen. When her daughter sat down, Gramwitch asked her, "What do you think about wearing slickers?"

Personally, Scarey enthused, she would love a pretty silky-looking slicker with ruffles around the neck and cuffs. "If it was roomy enough, I could spread the skirt over my broom and my cat Mehitabel. Then we all could fly warm and dry."

Gram rubbed her nose. "I suppose I should conjure up a water-repellent material."

"Yes, and include enough so I can make covers for our hats."

Gramwitch busied herself conjuring black slickers for herself and Scarey, and a tailored dark green one for her grandson.

"My, haven't we had an exciting evening?" Scarey trilled.

Witchard confessed he had forgotten to tell them something. "I have been chosen to be one of the Wise Men in the school Christmas play. I need a costume."

Scarey said quickly to her mother, "Let me conjure up something important for a change."

Gramwitch consented. She approved of her grand-

son playing the part of a *wise* man. Making the costume was not difficult. All Scarey had to do was mumble magic words and snap her fingers. A perfect costume arrived in moments. In one pocket was the false beard to stick on Witchard's chin.

Several days later Witchard brought home a hand-lettered invitation to the program. Gramwitch exclaimed, "Witchit! We have too many Christmas decoration lights to short-circuit at shopping centers."

Witchard frowned. "You're going to tamper with Christmas decorations? That's not nice."

"All we do is make them flicker a little. You know we never damage anything."

Scarey giggled. "Sometimes we scramble the music so "Jingle Bells" and "Rudolph the Red-nosed Reindeer" play at the same time!"

"Doing that is more important than seeing me act the part of a wise man?" Witchard complained. "I'll be the only one whose family isn't there. You haven't even met Mr. Abbott. Of course, he knows my folks are away. He probably thinks I'm an orphan."

"Oh, dear." Scarey was shocked. "We can't have that! We must attend the program, Mama. But what will we wear?"

"Not our witch uniforms. People mustn't know we're witches," Gramwitch said.

"We don't have a car. We'll have to use broom transport."

An idea sprouted in Witchard's mind. "Why not polish your silver buckles and wear your slickers? That way you won't have to change. Nobody wears hats indoors, so you'll have to do something with your hair." When he spied his grandmother's temper rising, he added, "Just for this one night. All the lady teachers wear makeup and pretty dresses."

Scarey confessed she had always wanted to wear lipstick. "Does it come in different flavors?"

Witchard told her the girls in his class used the same color·on their lips and fingernails.

His aunt studied her long black nails. "I think we'd better conjure up black silk gloves to cover our nails. But I still want red lipstick." Seeing that Gramwitch disapproved, she said, "We want to look stylish so Witchard will be proud of us, don't we?"

The old crone gave in. "Oh, all right!" She had to conjure up brushes so she and her daughter could smooth the snarls from their hair. The next night they experimented with several hair styles. Finally they both brushed their hair back into smooth rolls at the backs of their heads. This did not interfere with wearing their pointed hats while brooming to and from the school.

The night of the program, they flew to the school parking lot, parked their brooms in a shadow, and entered the building. Mr. Abbott greeted them. Witchard hardly recognized him. Instead of the usual jeans, plaid shirt, and boots, the teacher wore a suit, white shirt, and tie, and had waxed his mustache. He won Gramwitch's heart by complimenting her on having such a brilliant grandson. Then he escorted her and

Scarey to seats in the auditorium. Witchard went to his classroom to change into his costume.

Mr. Abbott smiled at Scarey. "After the program, it will be my pleasure to escort you two lovely ladies to the cafeteria for refreshments. Since you do not know other pupils' families, I will see that you meet them."

The program delighted the witches. They laughed every time Witchard's false beard fell off and he pressed it back on his chin. During the refreshment hour, Gram had a problem chewing the cookies. "I should have worn false teeth."

Her daughter agreed. "Try not to flash your fangs. The little children are staring at you."

The families they met wished them a Merry Christmas.

Gramwitch wished them a very Merry Christmas. When the crowd thinned out and Mr. Abbott was not looking their way, they turned invisible. Once astride their brooms, they flew home, whistling carols all the way.

School had closed for the holiday so Gramwitch had programmed Witchard back into a night flier. The three sat before the fire, rocking and chatting happily.

Gramwitch was in such rare good humor that Witchard risked telling her about his bold, new plan. "What day do we fly to the regional convention?"

45

He knew it would be held in a deserted barn near Pueblo, Colorado, a central location for most western members of OAW.

"We broom off Christmas night before air traffic becomes congested. Why do you ask?"

Witchard called up extra courage before revealing, "You might as well know I am going to make a speech at the convention."

Gram cackled rudely. "Come, come, come! Children never address the convention. They are there to be seen, not heard."

"My speech is pretty exciting. Don't you want to know what I will be saying?"

Suspicion sprouted like mushrooms in the old crone's mind. "I've watched you do your homework, but I never guessed you were preparing a speech. Of course, I want to hear it—even if you're not going to be allowed to give it. Proceed." When he hesitated, she urged impatiently, "Speak out!"

He had seen her stiffen like a cat waiting to pounce on an unsuspecting mouse. "It's only fair to warn you. I—I plan on doing something you might not like."

"Go on."

Witchard wondered if boldness might mask his jittery nerves. "I could do it without telling you, y'know," he reminded her. Then he relented and said, "I don't want you upset, or worrying about me, Gram. I want to share my plan with you and Scarey."

Gramwitch shook her finger at him. "Let me warn you, young wizard. You better not embarrass me at the convention."

Her grandson was truly shocked. "I would never do that. What I plan to do might make you famous. Sort of."

"Eh? How?"

"Well, I am going to announce at the convention that I plan to stow away on the new experimental space shuttle, *Sweeper*, which lifts off December 27. I'll be the first Junior Wizard in all witchdom to orbit the Earth!"

5

No Tricks on a Shuttle

"You w-h-a-t?"

Gram's screech caused bits of plaster to rain down from the ceiling.

Witchard gripped his rocking chair, in case she blew him back to his bedroom.

His grandmother built up so much pressure she almost exploded. At the last second she throttled back, and shouted, "Impossible! I forbid it! Now or ever!"

Like all witches who watched Spacevision programs about moon walks and shuttle missions, she knew some of the perils facing space travelers. She ranted on, "You are not going to expose yourself to below-zero temperatures, deadly radiation, fearsome winds, and darkness deeper than you see on your night flights."

Witchard argued that the Pioneers knew about those perils, but didn't let the hazards of space travel keep them home. They used their magic to protect themselves. "I don't have that much power, so I have to fly inside an orbiter. But I'll be as safe as the astronauts."

Gramwitch stamped her feet three times. "No, no, no! Besides, you're too young to bat around space."

Witchard was so relieved not to be blown down the hall, he grinned. "I think it would be great fun. Don't you want me to be famous so you can brag about me?" He eyed her. "You're mad because I didn't ask your permission. Well, I'm old enough now to do some things on my own. You better stop bossing me so much, or I'll run away!" He shook a finger at her. "You haven't even asked why I want to ride that shuttle."

Gram acted as if a thunderbolt struck her. "Don't you talk to me that way, young wizard."

"If I was the first to do it, I'd earn a gold medal."

Scarey understood. "Mama, you have forgotten young wizards are adventuresome, and resent being treated like toddlers. Be proud our young man wants to bring honor to his family."

The possibility of Witchard being awarded a gold medal by The Supreme cooled Gramwitch's anger. How she would love to show off a gold medal to her sister witches when they flew in for hot brew the first Thursday evening of every month. "You're right. If all goes well, he might be admitted to OWE, the Order of Witch Explorers. No junior has ever qualified for membership."

Then her pride crumbled before her love for her grandson. "No, I still forbid it. No gold medal is worth the risk. I couldn't live without . . . I mean, I can't approve your being away from home so long."

Witchard relaxed. He never doubted she loved him, even if she rarely said so. Now he realized that underneath her bossiness lay tons of love. "I wouldn't be alone, Gram, and the mission only lasts five days. Two astronauts and two mission specialists will be along. I'd be as safe as they are."

The old crone rubbed her nose some more. She suspected she had not heard the whole story. "You've got something else up your sleeve, haven't you?"

He exclaimed excitedly, "You guessed!"

Gram hadn't, but nodded.

Witchard tried the old trick of swap-and-trade. "I won't tell you anything more until you promise to help me."

Scarey laughed. "I'll help."

Gramwitch hedged. "You want me to program you into an astronaut."

"Hunh-uh. Guess again."

"The National Aeronatuics and Space Administration allows no one under eighteen to fly a mission. Or is it twenty-one? I forget which."

Witchard hummed a couple of notes. "There are ways of getting around even NASA's rules."

His grandmother snapped at his hint like a frog at a fly. "Do you know how?"

Knowing how cunning she was about promises, he insisted, "Promise you won't pull any of your old tricks on me. Or new ones."

She promised on her sacred oath.

Satisfied, he announced proudly, "I think I have figured the easiest, simplest way to contact our Pioneers."

The idea was so stupendous the two witches were speechless.

"Please sit back and listen while I try to explain. And Gram, please don't interrupt or argue about everything I say. Give me a chance. What I have to tell you is very complicated."

He took a deep breath. "See, for a long time I've been disgusted with our pokey research committee. The—"

Gram sat bolt upright and reminded him children did not criticize their elders. The research committee was made up of the most brilliant wizards and witches in the OAW.

Witchard groaned. "Why try to talk when you challenge everything I say? I should have known!" He stood up. "I'm going to bed."

"Sorry," Gram apologized. "I'll try not to butt in again."

Knowing his grandmother was impatient to hear him talk, he began again. "Okay. I'm disgusted with our research committee. The only proposals it made to The Supreme was for witches to put their own satellite in orbit, and bounce messages from it to outer space. Sure, we could magic a satellite into orbit—at least, I think we could if enough of us put our hats together—but why do that when you don't have to?"

Both witches appeared puzzled.

"Just about everybody agrees now that something blocks the messages we transmit up to the Pioneers, and the ones they promised to transmit down to us. Right?"

The two crones exchanged uneasy glances.

"Don't worry, I've heard the talk on WF about the Pioneers being lost in space and never coming back. But I don't believe it! I'm positive they're out there, and we'll be able to talk to them and they to us, once we remove the block."

Gramwitch could not remain silent another second. "And you think you know how to remove the block, or whatever it is?"

"Yes, ma'am."

"How?"

Witchard grinned. "Here's where my plan gets complicated. First, I'd stow away on the shuttle. Then, when the crew is asleep—I might have to magic them into deep sleep so they wouldn't wake up and see me—"

Gram said, panting, "I'll see you have power to do that. Go on!"

"That would help! Now, one of the *Sweeper* astronauts got permission to bring his amateur shortwave radio on board, and on his free time talk with ham operators around the world. Well, I already know how to magic our WF set so I can listen in on their transmissions down here. Why wouldn't I be able to magic his set to WF, and transmit to outer space where the Pioneers are? Any witch could do that."

Gramwitch pursed her lips and scratched her chin. "We don't know if our magic works in space."

"That's why I have to ride the orbiter and try some of our easier tricks, like buckle flash-talking, and going invisible. It's worth stowing away just to find out something like that. Then, if I can talk to the Pioneer . . ." He paused, his eyes sparkling. He'd let Gram and Scarey imagine for themselves what a marvelous accomplishment that would be.

Scarey had a question. "You wouldn't be tampering

with the communications system the astronauts use? Not tampering, exactly. Fiddling, I guess."

Witchard raised his right hand. "I promise not to fiddle with anything on the flight deck. I'll probably have to slip on the astronaut's headset—you know, the earphone and microphone thing—but it should be the same as the one I'm using."

"And you really think your plan will work? Oh, my, just the thought of your talking to Dearie and Darrell gives me heart flutters. Oh, dearie me, I hope they're all right. I don't know whether I can stand the suspense. Suppose they're . . . they're . . ." She couldn't go on.

"We've got to know," Witchard pointed out. "I'm not willing to spend the rest of my life wondering what has happened to them. I've got to *know*. If they aren't coming back, I want to *know*."

Scarey agreed it would be better if all the families of the Pioneers knew the truth. "But what if—"

Witchard confessed he had thought of a thousand "what ifs." "Look, the astronauts and Mission Control at Houston communicate on what they call downlink and uplink, regular but separate frequencies, *down* to Houston and *up* to the orbiter. I'll use what I've decided to call the E.T. link. The extra-terrestrial link. Orbiter-to-outer space."

"Naturally! But what if those Houston fellows listen in?"

Witchard giggled. "They can't. They're not witches. They don't know about our WF, and they can't understand our language."

In spite of age and arthritis, Gramwitch bolted out of her rocker. She danced Witchard around the kitchen. Scarey joined in, and Tom leaped on his master's shoulder. Soon Gram collapsed, out of breath. "Oh, I can't wait for you to pull tricks on that crew and the orbiter."

Witchard was horrified. "You're on the wrong track. Except to make the crew sleep sounder and use the astronaut's radio, which is no part of the orbiter, I'm not interfering with anything. I'm not flummoxing one single switch. How would you feel if I caused a horrendous disaster?"

Gram hadn't thought of that. "We pull lots of innocent tricks, but we're never destructive. All right, no tricks. Now tell us how we can help."

Witchard had a list memorized. "I'll need extra magic power to turn invisible up there, and put the crew into deep sleep for a few hours, and maybe enough to open a cupboard if I need a hiding place." He'd better have food pills like the Pioneers ate when they took turns on guard and WF duty. "Do you think I dare raid the orbiter pantry? Oops, I forgot. Pantry is the wrong word. The pantry on the *Sweeper* is part of the galley."

When Scarey said raiding the galley was stealing, he agreed to rely on the food pills. "Unless I see nice snacks going to waste."

Gram cackled. "Snacks are fair game. Tell us more about the *Sweeper*. We haven't seen it on Spacevision."

"That's because all the attention has been on the *Columbia* with the big Spacelab on it that came down in early December. *Sweeper* is like it, only its mission is to sweep up discarded space junk and grind it into a fine powder in a grinder set in the cargo bay. The powder will be dumped in treated waste water before being emptied overboard.

"I've read tons about it. The school librarian let me check out *The Space Shuttle Operator's Manual*. I programmed page after page in my brain. I know good places to hide." He smacked his forehead. "I almost forgot. I need astronaut's coveralls and microgravity shoe attachments."

Gram jabbed that request like a robin pecking at a worm. "You'll wear your green uniform! You'll be on witch duty."

He frowned. "There you go, bossing before I explain. I'll be wearing my greenies part of the time. But what if I can't turn invisible inside the *Sweeper*? Suppose someone sees me? If I'm wearing regulation blues, they won't pay any attention to me."

"Regulation blues?"

"Coveralls. I need the microgravity attachments to slip on over my shoes. They help you stick to the floor, instead of floating around. You float around when you're in a state of weightlessness when you're in space." He laughed. "You don't even need your broom to float. I'll show you sketches in the manual."

Scarey was so hyped up with pride and joy she exclaimed, "You are a genius! Your plan is glorious! The Supreme has to know about it. Mama, she might invite Witchard to say a few words at the regional convention. You might inspire others to accompany you."

"No-o-o!" he wailed. "The *Sweeper* isn't like the Pioneers' space bus. Or a school bus. And the last thing I want is a flock of tricking witches on board. All they'll do is make trouble, and keep me from doing what I told you. Talking to the Pioneers is my secret goal. I'm not going to share it with anybody."

"Aren't you one little bit scared?" Scarey asked. "I'd be scared right out of my hat."

Witchard was amazed. If the astronauts weren't scared, why would he be? "The lady astronaut didn't look scared when we saw her on Spacevision. She was laughing. And none of the crew of the *Columbia* got uptight when computer problems delayed their return to Edwards Air Force Base in California. It glided in without a hitch."

Gram waved him to be quiet. "I've been thinking about Scarey's suggestion. Any project this momentous should be reported in advance to The Supreme. Call her on the WF, Witchard, but I'll do the talking."

Witchard gulped, but did not move.

"Go on. Do as I ask."

He confessed he had already talked to The Supreme.

"You what? That's against the rules."

He smothered a giggle. "No, it isn't. You just made that up."

When Gram started breathing heavily, Scarey pleaded, "Stay calm, Mama, or you'll have a stroke." She asked her nephew nicely, "What did The Supreme say?"

"She said she was happy I called, and to go ahead with my plans, and . . . and I could tell about it at the convention."

Scarey eyed him. "You're holding back something. I can tell. Did our Supreme really give you permission to proceed?"

Witchard sighed. "I can go as long as someone goes with me."

Gram cackled shrilly. "That's no problem. I'm too old to go, and I wouldn't trust anyone outside the family. So it's your duty, daughter dear. You keep Witchard company. That way we'll keep all the fame and glory in the family."

6

The Big Speech

The flight to the regional convention in Colorado was routine. Leaving their cats to guard their home inside and out, the three witches lifted off at dark on a clear cold Christmas night. Since they flew at low altitude, their passing was not detected on radar.

The deserted barn chosen for the convention headquarters was comfortable. Hospitality Committee members had used their magic to make it warm and dry. They soundproofed the walls so the noisy proceedings would not attract earthlings seeking a rock festival. They conjured up rockers for all, knowing witches dislike straight chairs. If uncomfortable, they would be ornery, argue shrilly, and delay the voting. Several temporary fireplaces accommodated individual state caucuses and committee gatherings.

As Gramwitch took her place she warned, "Remember, young wizard, our family reputation is at stake.

Even I have never addressed this convention. Guard well what you say."

Scarey whispered in his ear, "Don't let a barn full of cranky old witches make you nervous."

The wail of a siren warned the delegates the convention was to begin. All seated themselves to watch the color guard march in, followed by the white-robed Supreme and her purple-caped officers.

Lengthy sessions punctuated with crotchety arguments followed. Annual reports were read, complaints aired, and new regulations passed. Finally The Supreme asked for attention."Next on the agenda is a brief speech by a Junior Wizard. I gave him permission to speak because I approve of what he plans to do. Listen, brothers and sisters, to what he says."

Witchard rose from his rocker. Gramwitch tucked in his shirt before he stepped up on the platform and walked to the center. He faced his audience, and smiled shakily. Since his knees were knocking loudly, he began, "That funny noise you hear is caused by my knees knocking. Will somebody please magic them to stop?"

The witches cackled, and clapped their bony fingers. Witchard won their favor by confessing he was properly scared to face those whose power he respected. Immediately his knees stiffened, so much so his legs felt like stilts. He cleared his throat, and thanked The Supreme for the honor of addressing the gathering. "Distinguished witches and wizards, officers of OAW, and Gramwitch." He chortled. "I always need her permission to speak."

Again the audience cackled and clapped. The delegates approved of a young wizard giving proper credit to his grandmother. She rose, waved so everyone could see her, and sat down.

Briefly Witchard identified himself as the son of Dearie and Darrell who had departed on the pioneering expedition into outer space. "For two years I have been a day witch attending a public school. I have learned a lot about outer space, and the missions carried out by space shuttles like *Challenger* and *Columbia*.

"Because I am determined to contact my folks, and calling them from our home transceiver hasn't worked, I plan to stow away on the first flight of the new shuttle, *Sweeper*. While the crew sleeps, I'll slip onto the flight deck and tune a transceiver there to our WF. Then I'll call the Pioneers on what I call the E.T., or extraterrestrial, uplink. I figure messages transmitted from almost two hundred miles above the Earth have a good chance of being heard by the Pioneers and"—he paused before shouting—"and answered!"

For a few seconds the hall was extremely quiet. Then the walls vibrated as the delegates shouted excitedly. A few tossed their hats in the air. The Supreme had to raise her hand for quiet so Witchard could continue.

He confessed he did not guarantee his idea would work, but was worth trying. "Even if I fail, I can conduct other experiments to add to our knowledge about the effect of weightlessness and orbiting on witches and their magic powers.

"In conclusion, I have to say something I didn't rehearse before Gramwitch. I know young witches never address a convention, but I have to say I think Senior Witches have been discriminated against. Not one of you has been invited to join the astronauts' corps, or serve as mission specialists, or even be observers. It's time you took your rightful place up there. Maybe I can open the way a little. Witches should be in space. The sky was ours for centuries!"

The wind stirred by their applause almost blew him off the stage. Finally he managed to say, "Thank you! Listen in on my transmissions from the *Sweeper* to Gramwitch. If I do contact the Pioneers, you will know right away. Tune in! I will talk more about the trip on the WF after I get home. Tune in then, and ask questions. I'll answer as best I can. And please wish me and my companion lots of luck. We'll need a barrelful!"

Bowing to The Supreme and the audience, he marched stiff-kneed back to his rocker.

"Well done," Gramwitch whispered. Scarey hugged him so his hat was knocked askew.

Wisely The Supreme announced a thirty-minute break for refreshments. She knew her people were frothing to discuss the young wizard's bold plan.

Gramwitch hopped to her feet. "I'm hungry. Let's eat." She dashed off with Scarey and another witch.

Happy to be left alone, Witchard closed his eyes. No one had flummoxed or hexed him. Still, some cranky old crones who hated youngsters were sure to resent a junior speaking out. As soon as the convention adjourned and he stepped outside the hall, they'd give him a pinch or jab.

He smiled craftily. By then he would be out of reach! He and Scarey planned to go invisible during the Grand Procession of seniors with fifty or more years of haunting-and-scaring to their credit. Gramwitch approved, and agreed no one would be watching them.

Now that the time for the speedy getaway to Cape Canaveral was little more than an hour away, Witchard's heart thumped faster.

Suddenly, from behind his left ear, a sweet young voice cooed, "Congratulations, Witchard. Your speech was fab."

He turned his head and looked into the green eyes of a young witch. Since she wore a dark green dress and hat, he knew she was the same rank as he was. For a mini-second he wondered if she had leg problems until he realized she was wearing long green leg warm-

ers, like the girls in his class at school. He cleared his throat. "Were you speaking to me?"

The attractive Junior Witch smiled, showing pearly white teeth. "Who else? We're practically alone. Your aunt grabbed my aunt and led her off to the refreshment table. She did it on purpose. I am supposed to tell you something."

Memory clanged between his ears. This was the only other Junior Witch living in Oregon. "You're Witcheena, from Eugene."

She nodded, her eyes flashing pretty sparkles.

Witchard's eyes shot off a few bold ones. "You've sure changed. Last year you looked like a real witch." He raised his eyebrows. "When did you start washing your face and combing your hair?"

"When I started wearing braces and was allowed to spend Saturday afternoons with earthling girl friends at the park. You've probably forgotten I'm a Resident Witch. In fact, I was the first one."

As the official Resident Witch for a large amusement park near Eugene, two hundred miles south of Witchard's home, she lived in a Witch House built in the trees shading the campground. Boys and girls camped overnight there. While they sang and toasted marshmallows, she flitted around on her broom, making witchy sounds.

His cheeks flushed when he recalled Witcheena had

66

been awarded a gold medal for originating Resident Witch duties as a new career for Junior Witches. He changed the subject. "What are you supposed to tell me?"

She chirped excitedly. "I'm going on the *Sweeper* with you."

Witchard spun around and glared over the back of his rocking chair. "Says who?"

"Your aunt and grandmother." When his jaw sagged, she warned, "Let me explain. Your aunt dreaded going on the *Sweeper*. She begged to stay at home. Your grandmother wouldn't listen at first, so in despair Scarey called The Supreme. She said that making you have a Senior Witch along would cramp your style. Also she said it was time junior-rank witches be allowed to carry out new ideas on their own. They don't need baby sitters. They shouldn't be treated like they were still witchlings. Having an old witch along would spoil the fun. Right?"

Witchard agreed heartily. "What did The Supreme say?"

"She agreed! She suggested I take your aunt's place."

"Why you?" he asked bluntly.

"Why not me?" she snapped. "We're the same age. We're from the same state. We both have parents with the Pioneers. And I have a gold medal already for doing something original and daring."

"Oh, snails," he muttered under his breath. The last thing he wanted was a tagalong who already had a gold medal. But if The Supreme ruled that Witcheena should take Scarey's place and Gramwitch agreed, he had to accept her.

"Scarey is telling my aunt right now, and I promise you Auntie won't make a fuss. Scarey will see that her slicker and coveralls are switched to my broom. I don't have a slicker or coveralls of my own."

Before Witchard could grumble, the siren snarled briefly. "Here come our families. Okay, we vanish during the procession, and meet outside by the pump." He turned and sat down.

When his aunt and grandmother joined him, Scarey whispered, "Did you have a nice talk with Witcheena?"

He glowered at her. "You could have told me."

"I didn't want you to know what a coward I am. Truly, darling, I would have withered away from fright."

"It's okay. Witcheena and I will get along fine as long as she realizes I am the commander of our expedition."

"Shhh!" Gram hissed. "The Supreme has called for order."

The meeting droned on for an hour. At long last The Supreme announced the concluding ceremony, the Grand Parade of the most elderly veterans. Gramwitch rose, hugged Witchard, and moved toward the center aisle. Scarey remained in her rocker because she was not elderly enough.

The marchers lighted candles and formed a long line. As the leaders moved toward the platform, Scarey said, "Now!"

Witchard and Witcheena went invisible and slipped through the wooden door without tearing their uniforms. Their brooms were waiting. Witchard ordered, "Tighten your chin strap. Here we go! Next stop Cape Canaveral!"

Their brooms streaked full speed toward the eastern horizon.

7

A Victory Dance

Before daylight the brooms touched down on a sand dune capped with tall beach grass at Cape Canaveral, where all U.S. manned space flights were launched. The exhausted passengers burrowed into the warm sand and pulled the grass over themselves. Now they were invisible to air patrols flying day and night over a twenty-mile stretch of the John F. Kennedy Space Center and the launch complex. The latter was located between Florida's Intercoastal Waterway and the Atlantic Ocean.

In spite of the sound of waves thrumming onto the beach nearby, and the mosquitoes, they fell asleep.

Witchard wakened shortly before sunset. Since he thought of himself as commander of an important expedition, his first duty was to inspect the area. Cautiously he rose to his knees and peered over the grass. The sandy beach on his left was deserted. The view

to the south took his breath away. The photographs
he had studied gave him no real feeling for the enormous size of the large vehicle assembly building where
the orbiter, solid rocket boosters, and external fuel tank
were joined for lift-off.

Eastward he scanned the launch complex and its
network of iron gantries supporting the spacecraft. From
his position the *Sweeper* looked trim, graceful, like a

71

bird straining to fly. He feasted his eyes on the glistening white space ship.

A lump swelled in his throat. When lift-off occurred in a few hours, he would be on board!

"Witcheena! Wake up and see the *Sweeper* before sunset."

She rose cautiously, yawning and blinking. "Ooooh," she murmured. "It's so beautiful."

Suddenly she threw her arms around his neck. "I'm so glad to be here."

Witchard jumped back like a scalded cat. "Glad you came."

He hoped he sounded laid back, the way Ted and his other pals did when they talked with girls. "See those windows near the top? That's the crew compartment where we'll be. Below it is the cargo bay. It's below now because the orbiter is poised on its end, called the aft fuselage. In orbit the craft is horizontal and the cargo bay is *behind* the crew compartment. Understand?"

Witcheena held one hand palm-side down, and then lifted it to a vertical position. "Got it."

He added importantly, "The vertical stabilizer, engines, and rockets are in the aft fuselage. Got that?"

She smiled sweetly. "You are so smart, Witchard."

His ego stretched. "Well, I should know something after all the hours I studied the shuttle operator's manual. It was a real grind."

Like her companion, Witcheena did not need binoculars to see distant objects. "I spy workmen riding up an elevator alongside the orbiter. Is that how we're going to reach the *Sweeper*'s door?"

"Hatch, not door," he corrected her. The elevator resembled an open-air cage. It rattled up and down within an iron framework, transporting workers and supplies to a walkway which gave access to the hatch, or side opening.

"The launch pad will be floodlighted after dark. Not that it matters. We'll go invisible and fly straight to the hatch."

The cloudless sky inspired her to stretch her arms, and inhale deeply. "Wouldn't it be nice if witches had their own vacation resort in a quiet place like this? Honestly, I don't want to move to another planet. Do you? I don't want to leave my work and my friends, even though I like to escape smog and noise every once in a while."

As blue and violet shadows blurred the ground, the orbiter glowed like a pillar of fire in the rays of the setting sun. Witchard saw the wistful look on the young witch's face. "A vacation resort is a great idea. Tell The Supreme. If wild birds can have a refuge, why not witches?"

Immediately he bit his tongue. Dumb ox! Why tell her to talk to The Supreme, who'd probably award her another gold medal!

Witcheena sat cross-legged on the sand and gazed up at a star gleaming faintly in the darkening sky. She chanted softly, "Star light, star bright, first star I see tonight. I wish I may, I wish I might, have the wish I wish tonight."

Witchard's resentment vanished. Sitting beside her, he said, "I bet we have the same wish. You want to contact your folks, don't you? I'll do my best, but don't be mad if I fail."

Just then the sun disappeared, and a dark quiet settled over the Cape. Then brilliant beams of light from several powerful floodlights illuminated the shuttle. Witcheena thought it would be fun to flummox the lights. "Can we go now?"

"We're not to flummox anything. The Supreme's orders. It's too soon to go now." There were too many workmen around, he explained. There might be a short time later when the guards and workmen on the job now would quit work and another shift came on duty. "Not that it matters too much. We'll go invisible, and I know where to hide inside."

"Where?"

"In the bunks. Guess what? The bunks are called *sleep restraints*. They're equipped with mattresses and sleeping bags but you have to buckle seat belts over yourself to keep from floating around. That's because, in orbit, you're in a state of weightlessness."

74

"Let's go now. I'm getting fidgety."

"No," he said firmly. "I'll decide when. Coming here was my idea. I did the studying. I say it's too soon to enter. We would have to stay hidden for hours before lift-off."

Both remained silent during a lengthy wait. Suddenly Witcheena recalled, "I forgot something." She pulled two small rolls of material from her dress pocket. "Your aunt conjured up pennants to pin on the tips of our hats."

Witchard was delighted.

The pennants were about eighteen inches long, and made of black nylon. They were emblazoned with the design of an owl, made of orange nylon. The owl was the official emblem of the Organization of American Witches. Overlaying its design were the letters O A W stitched in gold thread.

Witcheena pinned them on both hats. "Aren't they gorgeous? I feel so proud to wear one even if we'll be the only ones to see them. Now I'd like to change into my coveralls. Thank goodness, Scarey is small. I shouldn't have trouble wearing hers."

Mumbling and stamping, the two made their junior-grade uniforms whisk off and the coveralls settle in place. They were patterned after those worn by the astronauts when the atmospheric pressure inside the orbiter was similar to that on Earth. Smartly tailored of cobalt blue cotton cloth, they included a waist-length jacket, short-sleeved pullover shirt, and pants with patch pockets. These were closable to protect sunglasses, small tools, a pen and notebook, and the scissors needed to open food packets. A patch decorated with the American flag was sewn high on the left sleeve. On the other was a bright red circular patch lettered *Sweeper I*. An embroidered blue-and-white design pictured the orbiter sweeping fragments from a dark blue sky. The border was lettered with the names of the crew.

Witcheena wrinkled her nose. "Too bad our names can't be on there. Maybe I'll design one for witches to wear."

"After we return, maybe The Supreme will let us wear one."

One by one Witcheena examined the contents of each pocket. "A notebook and pen! Maybe I should write a book about our trip."

"I have to write a scientific report for The Supreme. It probably will be as dull as swamp water."

He watched Witcheena stretch, kick, and execute a few knee bends. "What are you doing?"

"Aerobics, since I'll be sitting so long. I want to get the feel of the coveralls." She flapped her arms and spun around. "I feel like a lady astronaut already."

Witchard located the plastic container of one-a-day

food-and-vitamin capsules in his jacket pocket. "Let's take one now, so it will digest before lift-off. And how about rolling up our witch uniforms and tying them on our brooms? We'll need our hats in order to fly."

Witcheena wondered what to do when they wanted to talk without having any of the crew hear them.

"Use your buckle-band communication. It's activated, isn't it?"

"I forgot about it."

When both attained their junior-grade rating, their copper shoe buckles were energized. By turning them slightly right or left, they could flash thoughts to other witches. They could communicate privately with one or two others without having every witch within two miles eavesdropping.

"We better make certain our buckles are working. Flash me a message, and I'll flash back."

Immediately Witcheena flashed silently in witch language, "Let's go!"

"Okay! Get ready," he responded. He knelt on Splinters' bristles. "Workmen are leaving the orbiter, so they must be going off shift. Wait until the elevator takes the last load down, and stays there until the new shift needs a lift. Then broom off."

Witcheena knelt on her broom, Cadenza, and grasped the broomstick tightly. "Oooh, I'm so excited!"

In about five minutes Witchard commanded, "Fly!"

Both witches turned invisible. Their faithful brooms rocketed skyward and delivered them safely onto the walkway leading to the *Sweeper*'s exterior hatch.

In spite of the fact neither they nor their brooms were visible, they hopped off their brooms and waved them like flags. They marched proudly along the walkway and entered the side hatch. Their new pennants flapped vigorously every inch of the way.

"Shhh!"

Until his eyes and ears assured him the orbiter was deserted, Witchard did not even breathe. Then he asked, "How about a victory dance?"

Witcheena grabbed his hands. "We made it! We made it!"

With hats bobbing, pennants flapping, and eyes shooting noninflammable golden sparks, the two danced a victory dance on the mid-deck of the *Sweeper*.

8

Takeoff Minus Five Hours

The dance had to be brief.

Witcheena gawked around the nine-by-twelve-foot room crowded with lockers. "Gee, you couldn't swing a cat in here. What is this? A storage room?"

Witchard laughed. "This is where the crew eats and sleeps. It's called the mid-deck. The flight deck would be above us if we were horizontal, in orbiting position. Everything is skeewunky because the *Sweeper* is poised on its aft fuselage. There's a storage deck under us full of containers and ducts distributing air and water.

"Let me point out some things before we dive into the bunks. Face the hatch. If we were horizontal, instead of vertical, the toilet would be on your left, then the hatch, and then the wash basin. When you want privacy, you pull that curtain along its track from the toilet to the washbasin."

Witcheena whooped. "I hope the hatch stays closed."

"It does. Okay, next to the washbasin is the galley where meals are prepared. Make a quarter-turn right and face forward. You're looking at a wall of lockers. Behind it is the avionics equipment, like electronic cables, miles of the stuff! Another quarter-turn and you're facing six bunks, stacked three high. That's called the sleep station."

He snapped his fingers. "No one will have time to nap or sleep until well after orbit, so I figured we would be safe hiding in bunks. Why don't we hide our brooms and hats now?" Witcheena had such a funny look on her face, he asked, "What's wrong?"

"We sleep standing up? Those bunks look like broom closets."

"Sure, because they're vertical. The pillow end is on the bottom. You have to raise that grilled privacy screen, which opens only halfway, and crawl inside. Watch." He got down on his hands and knees, removed his hat and tossed it and Splinters inside. "If you slip the tip of your broom under one of the restraint belts on the sleeping bag, it won't rattle around."

"But—"

"Don't argue now. We'll flash-talk later. Hide your broom first."

Witcheena patted her broom. "Be good, Cadenza." She tucked it and her hat out of sight, and closed the screen.

"Leave the screen open," Witchard advised. "We

might have to dive for cover in a hurry."

The Junior Witch looked very unhappy. "Where do we hide when the bunks are all in use? Hiding in them in the daytime could be risky. Suppose one of the astronauts wanted to take a nap? He might crawl in with you."

Witchard shrugged. "Go invisible."

"But what if we can't do that while we're in orbit?" She squinted through the doors of every storage compartment. "Look. There. The top row of lockers next to the bunks."

Witchard reached up and unsnapped the latches securing them. "There are extra sleeping bags stored in them. Maybe we should have more than one hiding place. We can each use one locker, and unroll the bags to put under and over us."

"Let's look in all the lockers while we can. You take one section and I'll take the other." After a few moments she exclaimed, "This one is full of food."

"And here's one stuffed with rescue bags. I read about them in the manual. They're for emergencies. I'll tell you about them later." As a precaution, he looked out the hatch. "The elevator cable is turning. Hide!"

"Which place?"

"The bunks. They'll be safer for lift-off. The crew stays on the flight deck."

Both crawled into separate bunks, stood up, turned

around and pulled down the screens. Witchard called out, "Can you see through everything into the flight deck?"

Witcheena could.

"Me, too. Talk about front-row seats. Gram would love this."

"I never had a front seat where I stood on a pillow."

"Never mind. Watch the elevator. And turn your buckle so we can flash-talk from now on."

The metal cage stopped level with the walkway. Three men clad in white coveralls stepped off and entered trough the hatch. They climbed a metal ladder to the flight deck.

Thumping sounds told Witchard his companion was trying to make herself comfortable. He leaned against the sleeping bag attached to a mattress which was fastened to a board. Cautiously he bent his knees until he could sit on the pillow with his legs crossed loosely before him. He flashed the information to Witcheena.

"Those men weren't astronauts, were they? They weren't wearing space suits."

Astronauts no longer wore bulky space suits for lift-off because shuttle flights had improved so much. However, they did need Snoopy-type safety helmets roomy enough to cover their headsets. "If you look up, you can see the commander's and pilot's seats have built-in life-support packs. The astronauts plug into them. And their seats have emergency ejection apparatus. The mission specialists pull out seats, and sit right behind them. Those bulky space suits and backpacks hang inside the airlock chamber between the middeck and Spacelab. They're worn only when the men work outside." The men they saw made up the handover crew. "They do the final checking, and hand over to the astronauts."

Both could see one of the crew lying on his back with his legs raised, and speaking from the flight commander's seat. "*Sweeper* calling Launch Pad and Ground Control. Do you read me?" His call was heard simultaneously by the Launch Pad supervisor close-by and also monitored by Mission Control in Houston, Texas.

The response was heard through a speaker set in the instrument console which separated the astronauts' seats. "Control reading *Sweeper*. Identify. Over."

Witchard broke out in goose pimples from head to toe. He couldn't believe he was hearing the conversations.

"Control, this is handover chief Pullian. Activating television monitor. Over."

Both witches watched Pullian hit a switch which lighted a small television screen set in the wrap-around instrument panels beneath the triple-paned forward thermal windows.

Ground Control announced, "*Sweeper*, you have three

minutes, twenty-nine seconds to T minus 5, beginning final countdown. Over."

Witchard flashed. "The letter T stands for takeoff. Minus 5 means takeoff time minus five hours. Got it? In three minutes, twenty-nine seconds it will be five hours to lift-off."

"That long?" Witcheena flash-wailed.

Witchard ignored her complaint. "The flight is computer-controlled from the Mission Control room at the Manned Spacecraft Center in Houston. The fellow we see in the left-hand seat has to be Pullian. Another man is in the pilot's seat on his right, and the third standing behind him. We can't see it from this angle, but there's an instrument panel and console across the back, or aft rear cockpit."

Both watched the handover crew turn switches on and off, check dials, and test hand grips used in flight maneuvers and docking. Soon Control announced, "*Sweeper*, you have T − 5, beginning final countdown."

Witchard flashed a cheer. "We're in business! Now is when they start filling the fuel tanks inside that big external tank."

"Big deal," Witcheena muttered.

"What did you say?"

"Nothing."

"Did you ever see so many switches? All it takes is

one light touch, and *va-room!* the main engines are ignited!"

Witchard concentrated on looking for the DAPS, the Digital Auto Pilot controls. There were two sets, one on the console between the commander and pilot, another on the aft crew console. His imagination ran riot. He saw himself pressing the DAPs to avoid a head-on collision with a gigantic asteroid, and then outmaneuvering a space pirate ship. *Zap!* He destroyed it.

Next he imagined he was invisible, standing behind the commander. Suddenly his power fizzled out. Witchit! There he was, exposed to the crew and the whole world because the television monitor was on. The fellows at Ground Control spied him. He could hear their frantic discussions. Was he a spy from an enemy planet, or a terrorist from Earth? Of course, they took so long arguing that his power recharged. He escaped by turning invisible again, and hiding where they couldn't find him.

At first he laughed until his ribs hurt. Then the laughs grew weaker as he sensed he might be in real danger. He looked around. The bunk had no life-support hookup! Or any sign of an individual oxygen tank. Without extra oxygen, he and Witcheena would black out during lift-off and might not recover!

Just then Ground Control informed Pullian, "*Sweeper*, you have T − 4:30 [takeoff minus four hours, thirty minutes]. Liquid oxygen tank now being filled. Over."

Pullian acknowledged, "Roger. We copy. Over."

Witchard's worries intensified. He wondered if he should flash Witcheena to turn invisible and escape while the hatch was still open. Then common sense told him to wait a little longer. Why flee now when he had at least three hours to find a solution?

Curiosity drew his attention toward the flight deck conversations. The crew reported: front panel switches, dials, and instruments checked; panel to left of commander checked; panel to right of pilot checked; overhead panel; aft crew station panels; aft console. "All switches now in normal operating position."

"You still there?" he flashed.

Witcheena replied, "Where else? I feel like a pretzel in a sardine can."

At T − 3 Ground Control stated, "Liquid oxygen tank filled. Liquid hydrogen tank now being filled. Over."

Witchard remembered that two separate tanks, connected by a corrugated intertank section, were located in the huge external tank only a few feet away. He hoped nothing went wrong in that area! "Only one more hour until the astronauts arrive!"

"I wish I'd brought my nail polish kit."

Every minute dragged until two handover crew members descended to mid-deck. They removed portable cushioned seats from a locker, fastened them to the floor, and sat down. Both took a little snooze.

At last the elevator lifted three men to the walkway. Witchard squinted to read their identification badges. The first to step out was the Launch Supervisor. Behind him came Colonel John McKenzie, the *Sweeper*'s flight commander, and Lieutenant Henry Ransome, the pilot. Both wore in-flight coveralls and helmets. They looked almost like twins because of their short dark hair. McKenzie carried a slim briefcase.

Witcheena came to life. "Witchee, are they ever handsome?"

Witchard guessed so. He was more excited about the briefcase. "It holds the flight code cards to be inserted in the on-board computer."

The elevator dropped down while the three climbed to the flight deck. The Junior Witches craned their necks to watch Pullian help the astronauts lie down on their seats with their legs raised, and adjust headsets under their helmets.

Four men arrived next. One carried a portable television camera on his shoulder. Another had three still cameras dangling from cords around his neck. According to their badges they were official NASA photographers. Behind them came Dr. Lester Browne and Dr. William Youngman. Witchard flashed that they were scientists, not astronauts. They would use the Remote Manipulator Arm installed in the cargo bay to retrieve burned-out space junk, and also conduct experiments in the Spacelab. They, too, wore in-flight coveralls, and climbed to the flight deck.

Witcheena giggled. "There wouldn't be room for us up there even if we went invisible."

Soon Ground Control ordered, "*Sweeper*, unstow cue cards. Over."

Colonel McKenzie removed the laminated cue cards from his case and placed them in a three-ring holder fastened to the console. In abbreviated form these provided the last-minute flight sequence programs. "Control, cue cards in place. Over."

Witchard's attention was distracted by a man entering the mid-deck with a fairly large cage in his arms.

"What have you got there?" one of the handover crew asked.

"Six white rats."

"Will they all survive lift-off?"

"You bet. The cage is self-contained, and sits inside a rescue ball equipped with portable oxygen." He opened the pass-through into the airlock and continued on to the Spacelab. After securing the cage and opening the oxygen gauge slightly, he left.

Seeing the cage and being reminded of the rescue bag almost bowled Witchard over. His problem was solved!

He flashed, "I goofed. We're going to have to move. These bunks don't have oxygen hookups. I just found out what to do. After everyone leaves and the crew is strapped in their seats, I'll pull a couple of rescue bags out of a locker. They come equipped with oxygen tanks and face masks. I know about them from the manual."

"What about our brooms and hats?"

Witchard snapped, "They don't need oxygen! We do! Get set. Those rescue bags are our only hope for a safe lift-off."

9
Lift-off!

The Flight Commander, Pilot, and Ground Control carried forward their routine duties. At T − 1:30 they began still another round of checking air-to-ground and air-to-air communications.

"Watch everything," Witchard flashed. "We should know which switches activate the uplink and downlink. I won't use them because they're not linked to WF, but I better know where they are in case of an emergency. I'm a bit worried. I didn't see Pilot Ransome carrying his ham radio. Maybe it's already on board."

"Roger, and don't be a worrywart," Witcheena flashed.

"Okay, Ride," he drawled, using the first woman astronaut's name. "From here on you're not my guest. You're my crew. I'll depend on you for help."

"Roger, Commander."

Commander. Witchard grinned. He liked that.

Finally the Launch Supervisor was satisfied everything was in order. He shook hands with the astronauts and scientists, secured to their seats, and departed with the photographers. Pullian backed down the ladder, noted his men had stowed away their folding seats and were waiting out on the walkway. A quick glance assured him everything on the mid-deck was secure for lift-off. He stepped outside and closed the hatch firmly. It would be locked in a computer-controlled procedure.

Witchard looked out the hatch window until the last man stepped into the elevator, and dropped from sight. "Time to move! Don't forget your hat!" he flashed.

Quietly he lifted the privacy screen, slid out of the bunk with hat in hand, and closed the screen. While Witcheena did the same, he stepped to the locker where he had spied the rescue bags. He removed two.

Witcheena retrieved the two folding chairs the hand-over crew had sat on, and secured them to latches recessed in the floor.

"We can whisper because everyone upstairs is wearing earphones. We'd better save buckle flash-power whenever we can."

Both examined the rescue bags. They were fashioned of insulated fabric, fairly roomy, and opened along a zipper.

"There's no room for our hats," Witcheena objected.

"No problem. We'll magic them smaller. Let me help

you unzip your bag." When it was fully open, she stepped into it and zipped it halfway up. The oxygen tank and face mask were inside a pouch fastened inside at the waist. "Okay. Now sit down and pull the bag over your hair. Then lie back."

He lifted her legs onto the cushioned leg rest and fastened the restraint straps across the knees and at her waist. "Scrooch around until you feel comfortable." Meanwhile he removed the tank and mask from their pouch and placed them on her stomach. "Slip the strap attached to the face mask over your head . . . now put on the mask . . . and now your hat."

"It's too big," she mumbled through the mask.

"Magic it smaller until it fits inside." After it shrunk, he guided her fingers to a tiny dial atop the oxygen tank. "To start the oxygen flowing into the mask, you turn this dial slowly. Not now! Later."

Ten seconds before lift-off, he said, the countdown would be placed on Hold if the astronauts needed to make a final check of something. "You'll hear Control announce when the countdown resumes. That's when you start the oxygen flowing. Got it?"

"I guess so," she replied nervously.

He closed the zipper, but left a tiny opening so the pennant could remain outside. "Got to fly in style. Can you see all right through the bag?"

"Roger."

"Once I get hooked up, we'll flash-talk. Brace yourself. I'm going to move a lever that raises the leg rest until your legs are at right angles to your hips." She did not complain as he made the adjustment. "Now you're all set for lift-off."

Assisting Witcheena helped him know how to speed his hookup. He raised the leg rest before closing the zipper, shrank his hat, and remembered to leave his pennant outside. Excitement and tension made him quiver from head to toe. The next time he saw Witcheena face to face, they would be in orbit!

At T − 0:0:10 (takeoff minus ten seconds) Control announced there would be no Hold. "*Sweeper*, you're looking mighty good. Go for launch. Over."

Witchard turned on the oxygen tank and flashed a reminder to Witcheena to do the same.

Control counted loudly, "Nine-eight-seven-six-five-four . . . we have main engine start . . . two-one-zero . . . Solid Rocket Booster ignition. Lift-off!"

Witchard experienced a strong forward jolt as the rocket boosters ignited. Having seen lift-offs on Space-vision, he was not frightened, but his pulse was racing. Enormous bolts of orange flames and steam burst from the base as the engines and rockets attained full thrust, and the *Sweeper* lifted off. Fire and smoke engulfed the launch pad, then billowed outward and skyward as the glistening shuttle escaped fire, earth-shaking thundering, and the planet Earth. Six seconds later it had cleared the tower.

The orange glare reflected in the mid-deck was blinding. Witchard had to close his eyes. Every bone, muscle, vein, and drop of blood in his body felt the tremendous thrust of takeoff. He inhaled oxygen in deep gulps. He felt as if the entire planet was pressing down on his chest, with giant pincers squeezing his ribs and drums hammering inside his head. He blacked out temporarily.

Two seconds later *Sweeper* rolled 120 degrees to the right, and climbed in a glorious arc into the night sky over the Atlantic. The thrust of the rockets peaked, and subsided. The main engines throttled back as computers controlled the acceleration rate to maintain a level below that of 3 g, or three times Earth's gravity.

In two more seconds the rockets burned out. Their empty casings separated from the orbiter and fell gracefully toward the ocean. Free of their weight, the orbiter gained speed and altitude.

At $T + 0:06:30$ (takeoff plus six minutes, thirty seconds) *Sweeper* was traveling fifteen times the speed of sound at an altitude of 80 miles (130 kilometers) above the Earth. Swooping and soaring in roller coaster fashion, it dove gradually to an altitude of 72 miles (120 kilometers). This prepared for separation of the external tank now nearly empty of liquid fuels.

On attaining a speed of 17,500 miles per hour (28,500 km) the shuttle's tendency to escape Earth's gravity slowly equaled the down-pull of Earth's gravity. Computer commands and the pilot's skill maneuvered the orbiter for a smooth entry into orbit 172 miles (277 km) above the Earth.

Meanwhile the atmospheric pressure inside the orbiter was adjusted so that it equaled that of sea level on Earth. The *Sweeper* had also changed from vertical to horizontal position. Had it not taken off in the dark, its crew could have looked out and down from the flight deck windows and seen their swiftly receding homeland. For the moment they sped on in darkness.

When Witchard opened his eyes, he saw that the mid-deck was lighted. The terrible feeling of pressure was almost gone, and in its place a peaceful floating sensation, a dreamy weightlessness. His joy was boundless as he overheard Colonel McKenzie announce, "Control, we have orbit at T + 0:47:12. Over."

10
Breakfast in Orbit

Witchard's first concern was for Witcheena. "Are you all right? Did you black out?"

She said yes to both questions. "Get me out of this contraption."

"Turn off the oxygen."

Quickly he unzipped his rescue bag, slipped off his hat and mask, and stored the mask and the oygen tank in their pouch. As he reached over and unzipped her bag, he asked, "How did you like lift-off?"

"It was fab, fab, fab!" she burbled. The moment her hat and mask were removed, she exclaimed, "Witchee! I'm sitting up."

Now that the *Sweeper* was in horizontal flight position, both were sitting with their legs out in front.

Witchard magicked both hats back to normal size and leaned forward to unsnap his leg belts. Witcheena gasped, "Your hat! Quick, grab it!"

Witchard's green pointed hat was drifting toward the ceiling. He smacked his forehead. "I forgot about weightlessness. Anything not tied down floats free." He tried to explode into action, only to discover immediately that no matter how fast he tried, he moved as if in deep water. The effects of being in a state of zero gravity, or weightlessness, made his body buoyant. His fingers felt like marshmallows. Worse, his arms, no longer confined inside the bag, took on a life of their own, and raised until they were at right angles to his body.

He sputtered, "Witchit! I've got to rescue my hat before it reaches the ladder opening and sails up into the cockpit."

By this time his hat was bouncing sassily along the low ceiling. He unfastened the belt around his waist and unzipped the bag its full length. Immediately his legs began lifting, too.

Wide-eyed, Witcheena giggled so hard she couldn't help him. "You look like a four-legged octopus!" She cackled loudly.

"Quiet!" he flashed, glowering at her. He glanced upward through the ceiling into the cockpit. "Thank gosh, zero gravity doesn't affect our vision. I can see the scientists folding away their seats. We've got to hide before anyone climbs down here. Give me a hand."

He bent his knees, dug his heels against the seat,

and tried to rocket off. Instead he rolled in a complete somersault, while the bag fluttered and curled upward. The loose ends of the belt straps unfurled like flower petals.

When Witcheena leaned forward, her hat wobbled away. Weightlessness did not slow her rapid thinking. Her responses were swift, even though her motions were slow. She grabbed her hat before it was beyond reach, plopped it on her head and snapped the elastic strap under her chin. Then she freed herself of the seat belts and bag, but wisely strapped one section of the belt around her left arm to keep herself from drifting.

"Yeow! Ow!" Witchard yelped as his head banged the low ceiling. He flailed his arms like a swimmer until he retrieved his hat. Then he discovered he could not lower himself. His exertions rolled him into another somersault.

Again Witcheena giggled so hard she was helpless. "Give me a hand!"

Steadied by the strap around one arm, she twisted one leg and managed to shove the toe of her shoe under the padded seat. Then she stretched upward to extend a hand to her floundering friend. She pulled him down until he floated at seat level, and grabbed a strap.

"Thanks," he grumped, shoving on his hat and securing the chin strap.

"No charge," she said, struggling not to laugh.

Breathing heavily, he muttered, "We've got to fish out those microgravity straps and slip them over our shoes. They're in our pants pockets." After another frantic glance up through the ceiling, "The scientists are standing up. Hurry!"

Somehow the two managed to pull out their plastic webbed shoe straps and slip them over the toes and around the heels of their shoes. The suction cups stitched to the underside of the straps gripped the floor solidly when they finally made contact.

When Witcheena took a step, she had to tug hard to free each foot. Once more she burst out laughing. "This is like walking in wet cement!"

"Dr. Browne's moving toward the ladder. Hide!"

"Bunks or overhead lockers?"

"Lockers. Grab your rescue bag."

Both babbled the proper magic phrase to make the locker latches unsnap, and the doors fly up. Within seconds both had leaped, rolled into the storage areas, and slammed the doors. The stack of lockers filled the space between the bunks and the large cylindrical air-lock chamber. The remaining cramped space in the corner of the aft wall was occupied by the toilet.

"We forgot to fold up our seats, and the belts are dangling," Witcheena flashed worriedly as she struggled to roll her rescue bag into a pillow.

"Too late now," Witchard replied as feet appeared descending the ladder.

Above, on the flight deck, the Commander and Pilot continued their duties and conversations via radio downlink and uplink with Mission Control at Houston. The two mission scientists unplugged their life-support systems, slipped on microgravity shoe attachments, unfastened seat belts, and stowed their seats away. This made room for them to stand in front of the aft console. They awaited the command to open the cargo bay doors which would prevent a fatal heat buildup inside the crew compartment.

Colonel McKenzie was blissfully unaware that two Junior Witches were hiding on board, and flashing messages in their witch language, which caused an unusual amount of static in the *Sweeper*'s reception. After reporting all was well, he remarked, "Control, we're receiving peculiar sounds on both uplink and downlink. Hard to describe. Not the usual static. We hear *dit-dit-dits* in patterns which suggest scrambled speech. What's going on? Are we hearing garbled computer commands? Or are someone's false teeth clicking?"

Ground Control ran a fast check. "Negative." Then someone drawled, "You boys getting high on too much oxygen? Turn on your exterior lights and look out. Maybe you got a UFO hovering close-by. Maybe it's trying to make contact."

The Colonel chuckled. "*Sweeper* will check." After his crew scanned the darkness with beamed lights, he acknowledged, "Sorry. No UFO or strange signals. Our lights off now. Will keep sharp lookout for alien craft."

Control drawled, "Roger. Permission granted to use RMA [Remote Manipulator Arm] to capture alien craft. If the crew looks like E.T., say 'Hello' and 'Peace,' and share your M&Ms."

The flight crew burst out laughing.

Soon Control ordered opening the long curved doors which formed the upper portion and ceiling of the sixty-foot-long cargo bay which extended from the crew compartment to the aft fuselage.

Immediately the two mission scientists, standing by the aft console, turned switches to illuminate the bay, and others to release thirty-two latches. Dr. Youngman raised and locked the doors in Open position. These would remain open until the *Sweeper* was positioned for re-entering the Earth's atmosphere.

With this important task completed, Dr. Browne remarked, "I drew chief cook and housemaid duties for today. Everybody want coffee?"

"Roger! The sooner the better!"

He stepped to the ladder and descended cautiously. When his shoes gripped the floor, he glanced around the mid-deck. "What the—?"

He was astonished to see the two spare seats still latched to the floor, and their belts swaying back and forth. However, other matters were more urgent. In two broad vaulting steps he leaped toward the Personal Hygiene Station [toilet]. The narrow three-sided cubicle, somewhat similar to those on commercial airplanes and buses, occupied the corner next to the exterior hatch.

Quickly Witchard magicked the seats so they popped free of their latches, folded up, and quietly slipped into their storage cupboard. "How about that?" he flashed. "Our magic works great in orbit! I don't want Dr. Browne telling the Commander someone had not put the seats away. The handover chief might be blamed, and get black marks on his record."

"I think you should give him a mild flummox so he'll forget he saw the seats."

"No way," Witchard flashed back forcefully. "Gramwitch and The Supreme made me promise not to tamper with the crew members' memories while they're in orbit. Our flummox might be too strong, and erase something they must remember."

Dr. Browne emerged from the Hygiene Station and walked to the small circular washstand built into one side of the galley. It was enclosed with plastic cuffs through which he thrust his hands to reach water and soap dispensers.

Witcheena was curious. "Where's the shower?"

There was none. So far engineers had not solved how to control a stream of water, small or large, from flying upwards and spreading throughout the orbiter. "He'll turn on a fan to draw the water he uses down into the waste water compartment. Instead of showering he'll use specially-treated wet wipes, and dry off on paper towels. His clean underwear and shaving kit are in his private locker. The men shave every day and try to look sharp because they're on television so much."

"Sally Ride didn't look like she used TV makeup."

Both watched while Dr.Browne washed and dried his hands as well as the wash basin, and shoved the damp towel into the trash bin set in the floor beside the galley.

When he turned and saw no seats in sight, he appeared astounded, then suspicious, quickly puzzled, and finally confused. He stepped over to the front of the galley to unfasten the top and bottom latches. Then he looked again at the now-empty space where he had seen the seats. He shook his head, and opened the doors.

Witchard whistled softly. The galley reminded him of the pop and sandwich machines at school. Numerous compartments held serving trays, silverware, pantry items, and a plastic bin of small packets containing liquid mustard, salt and pepper, catsup, or barbecue sauce. There was a convection oven, small sink, and hot and cold water injectors.

Dr. Browne clamped on a metal tray to provide counter space, and placed four plastic covered mugs on it. Tiny magnets held them in place. Each contained a premeasured amount of dehydrated coffee and slits in which to insert drinking straws. He injected boiling water through these, crimped them so they would not leak, and shook the contents vigorously.

Next he opened a drawer in the stack of storage bins at his right, and removed a package labeled Day 1 Snacks B.

Witchard squinted until he could read the label. "Day 1 means today. B stands for Breakfast. The food for each day's three meals and snacks is wrapped separately. That way whoever prepares the food doesn't have to wonder what to fix."

After cutting open the package, the scientist removed four granola bars. He didn't bother closing either the package or galley doors before carrying the tray up the ladder into the flight deck.

Witcheena inquired, "Could we snitch a granola bar? I'm starved."

"We aren't supposed to eat the crew's food."

"Who said so?"

"Gramwitch and Scarey."

"Not The Supreme?"

Not that he remembered. "All I promised her was that I wouldn't touch any switches or dials, or do anything that might cause a problem."

Witcheena smiled craftily. "Well, I didn't promise anybody anything. I'm a witch, and witches play tricks. And I should know whether my magic works on some trick like this. Here goes!"

She pointed at the snack pack, mumbled magic words, and tapped one shoe against the side of her hiding place. Immediately the plastic bag shook. One, and then another granola bar wriggled free, and drifted toward her. She opened the door on her hiding place, reached out, and grabbed both.

Witchard opened his door and watched glumly as she nibbled on the oatmeal-and-raisin cookie.

"Want one?"

He shook his head. "Can't. I promised."

Witcheena rolled her eyes. "You didn't promise not to accept a treat from me, did you?" When she waggled the cookie under his nose, he snatched it.

As the two munched happily, they looked about the mid-deck. Witcheena leaned out as far as she dared to examine the cylindrical airlock compartment. The crew entered the large metal drum when moving through it to enter the fifteen-foot-long laboratory installed in the cargo bay. The airlock was also used, Witchard explained, when the crew members prepared for EVA (extra-vehicular activity) outside the orbiter.

"I'm worried about the rats. I'm going to open this thingamajig, and go check on them," Witcheena announced.

Witchard was horrified. "You mustn't go in there yet. Dr. Browne or one of the others might see you."

Witcheena wrinkled her nose at him. She rolled out of her hiding place, closed the cover and flailed about until her hands grasped the metal bar handle on the airlock opening. "Toodleooo!" she flashed as she disappeared inside.

"Wait for me!" Witchard protested as he propelled himself after her.

II

Close Call in the Spacelab

Witcheena brushed past the bulky space suits and life-support backpacks hanging inside the airlock chamber, and opened the far hatch. She stepped into a small, compat, lighted laboratory. Recognizing the rescue bag similar to the one which covered her during lift-off, she moved toward it. While her shoe attachments held her to the floor, her arms floated as if she were flying. She grabbed at the counter on which the animal cage was latched. Zipping open the cover, she pushed it down on all sides and turned off the oxygen.

"Poor babies," she crooned. "You're all upset by that nasty old lift-off." She reached down and slid her left hand under one rat, lifted it out, and stroked its back gently. "I don't understand why rats are used on a shuttle mission."

"For behavioral experiments," Witchard told her.

"For what?"

"Our science teacher at school keeps mice on hand for us kids to observe. We take notes on how they behave . . . you know, if heat or light or noise affects their appetites." He pointed to a box fastened to the counter. "This is called a maze. See how its interior is divided into a complicated network of channels? You put a mouse, or rat, into one end and note how much time it takes to find its way through the labyrinth to the end, where it's fed a treat. These rats probably were tested at some lab at home, and the mission scientists will put them through the maze every day. By comparing the times it took them to run through before they experienced lift-off, and afterward, scientists can tell if being in space makes them slower or faster, or makes them more or less confused. That kind of information helps scientists understand the effects of space travel on humans."

The rat Witcheena petted had curled up on her hand, and gone to sleep. "Poor darling, it's exhausted." She slipped it into one of her jacket pockets, and chose another to pet.

"You must be used to handling rats."

She shook her hat. "Kittens, not rats. Auntie and I have twenty-six cats. We don't bother counting the kittens. I'm always doctoring them. After I become a

Senior Witch, I plan to be an animal doctor."

He grinned. "After this trip you might want to be a lady astronaut."

She shrugged.

Witchard looked out the windows overlooking the cargo bay. The darkness was so intense the exterior lights barely revealed the Remote Manipulator Arm, debris-crushing machine, and pallets stacked with payload experiment canisters.

"Let's go," he pleaded. "Someone is bound to climb down to mid-deck and wonder why the airlock hatch is open. We'll be discovered."

Witcheena made a face at him. "Honestly, you're so nervous you've forgotten all we have to do is go invisible." Privately she knew he was right in being alarmed, but wasn't about to say so. "All right. I'll put the rats back in the cage and zip the cover so no one will suspect we've been in here. Then we'll leave."

Witchard thought they should test whether or not they could go invisible. "We can't take our magic for granted. You go first," he suggested. "I'll close the hatches after us." Suddenly he yawned. "Invisible or not, we have to hide. Besides, I'm getting sleepy."

Witcheena did not lag. *Plink!* She turned invisible with no problem and headed for her hideaway. Once inside the storage locker, she stretched out on the rescue bag, covered her eyes with her arms, and fell asleep.

Witchard was much relieved to find he could turn invisible at will, and soon was sound asleep in his locker.

Shortly after, the two mission specialists descended to mid-deck. Both worked at preparing breakfast. One removed four packets of frozen sausages, scrambled eggs, and sweet rolls from a small freezer, and popped them into the convection oven. The other locked four individual serving trays onto a metal tabletop rolled out from between two large storage lockers built along the forward wall. He set cups of canned peaches and containers of grape drinks, small forks and spoons wrapped in napkins, and liquid seasoning packets on the trays.

The crew had to eat standing up. Weightlessness caused them to lean back whenever seated. Also, food adhered to the backs of forks or spoons as well as the fronts. Food covered with gravy or sauce had to be handled skillfully to keep their chins or jackets from being smeared.

Commander McKenzie joined the two for breakfast. He ate quickly so the pilot could take his first break since taking over from Pullian.

Control continued to order small maneuvers during each orbit. For these changes in speed, pitch, and altitide, the astronauts employed the OMS (orbital maneuvering system) engines, one forward and another aft. They also used the RCS (reaction control system), firing clusters of small rocket engines placed in the *Sweeper*'s nose and tail. To combine use of the two systems, they pressed DAP (digital auto pilot) controls.

During its ninety-minute orbits, flown at temperatures as low as 150 degrees below zero Fahrenheit, the craft occasionally pitched like a bronc, or yawed from side to side. All previous flights had experienced minor performance problems, mostly in electrical circuits, communications, or on-board computers. Thanks to the instant responses and the two back-up systems, no problems became life-threatening and could be corrected.

After breakfast the scientists spent the entire morning checking circuits in the laboratory, and also the twenty payload experiments mounted on pallets bolted to the counters. Whenever the orbiter flew in blinding sunlight, they doffed their jackets and put on sunglasses.

Dr. Browne removed the rescue bag from around the rat cage, and stored it and the oxygen tank under the counter. "Look at this!" he gloated. "All six sleeping like babies." Later he would place each rat in the plastic maze and note the time needed to find its way out.

Dr. Youngman, a physicist with much expertise in cosmic ray studies, calibrated rays reflected off sensor plates directed toward the sun. Later he activated a small camera to photograph movements of several gold-fish swimming in a covered tank. The experiment had been designed by high school students, who also raised the $3000 charge to have it placed on board. The tank, camera, and film would be returned to them so they could see the effects of weightlessness on fish.

When the men finished their morning duties sooner than expected, they tied cords from their belts around cupboard handles, curled up, and napped briefly.

Although Dr. Browne was designated "house-keeper" for the day, Dr. Youngman helped him prepare lunch. The afternoon passed in practicing use of the RMA (remote manipulator arm) by using hand-grips and switches on the aft console. They raised and extended its long metal jointed sections, or legs, and swung the end grip, or hand, up and out over the bay doors and back. At rest, the RMA resembled a huge robotlike grasshopper.

On Day Two, Day Three, and Day Four they would extend the arm, gather in fragments of burned-out and discarded space hardware whose exact location had been charted. The junk would be returned to the cargo bay. Some would be run through the crusher, and a few bits clamped to pallets for delivery to laboratories on Earth.

The Junior Witches did not waken until the crew

finished dinner. The astronauts' work log still called for two more hours at their stations on the flight deck.

Seeing the mid-deck was deserted, Witchard opened the door on his hiding place. For a moment he missed joining Gramwitch and Scarey for a mug of brew and family talk around the fireplace. He wondered if Tom missed him. His cheeks crinkled when he imagined how different things would be if Gramwitch was on board, and having her way. She wouldn't be there without her jar of brew powder, and somehow would conjure up a fireplace and nonflammable fire, and rocking chairs, probably in the storage deck under the mid-deck. He chortled. In no time at all his grandmother would be running the *Sweeper*.

Witcheena flashed, "You awake?" The latches on her hiding place snapped open, and she raised the door. Her hair was a mess, her eyes puffy from sleep. She lay on her stomach with her arms crossed and supporting her chin. "What time is it?"

"Six, six-thirty," he whispered. "Better swallow your food pill. The galley is closed."

She fished it out and managed to swallow it without drinking something. "How much longer do we stay cooped up? Can't we move into the laboratory?"

Witchard nodded. "Good idea. We can't sneak onto the flight deck until after the crew has gone to bed. Okay, let's move."

"Visible or invisible?"

"Visible. I need some exercise."

For the next hour Witcheena enjoyed herself petting and cooing to the rats. Witchard examined the varied experiments, without laying a finger on them. But he was restless. He did not like being cooped up, even in a space laboratory. Even though it was removed from the cockpit, he closed the hatch before speaking out in witch language. "Let's play ball, or something."

"Flash dancing would be more strenuous."

"I couldn't even learn how to do a grand right and left in square dancing." He peeled off several paper towels and wadded them into a ball. "Let's bat this back and forth like you do in volleyball. Every time one of us catches it, it counts one. First to score twenty wins the game."

Witcheena returned the rat she was petting to the cage, and locked the cover. "Ready!"

Tossing the ball was easy, although it waffled about instead of moving swiftly in one direction. Leaping to catch it was tricky because their shoe attachments made it impossible to jump quickly. Their body contortions were so ridiculous that both lost easy catches while turning somersaults or doubled up with laughter.

The sillier the game, the more they forgot to keep their voices down. Soon they called back and forth. When Witchard found himself head-down and buttocks bouncing along the ceiling, Witcheena squealed.

During their game the flight crew was enjoying a brief period of relaxation. Control transmitted a summary of world news and messages from their families. No one paid attention to the sounds issuing from the intercom because it was mixed in with static and voice-overs.

However, when they stood to stretch, a sudden burst of laughter and then the squeal startled them. The pilot punched switches to pinpoint the source. "Those sounds are coming from the lab."

Dr. Browne guessed the rats must be upset, or fighting.

"The lights are on, and I distinctly remember turning them off," Dr. Youngman exclaimed.

The pilot shrugged. "No sweat. We get gremlins in the circuits every now and then."

As more *dit-dit-dits* poured forth, Commander McKenzie laughed. "I'll be doggoned if that doesn't sound like human voices."

Pilot Ransome reminded him they could be receiving the relay station in the Australian outback. "Anybody recognize the lingo? Or is it Japanese?"

None had any familiarity with aborigine talk. The Commander knew some Japanese from military service in the Pacific. "No way is that Japanese."

"I'll check," Dr. Youngman volunteered.

Witcheena happened to be facing the airlock hatches when he opened the one on the mid-deck. "Somebody's coming! Go invisible!"

Both Witchard and Witcheena vanished before the scientist entered. Because of weightlessness, they drifted up against the ceiling. Dr. Youngman tested the wall switch and found it worked perfectly. The rats were calm and quiet.

He called toward the intercom, "How's the sound level? Are my words distorted?"

The pilot responded, "Level's normal. Shucks, you didn't find any little green men hiding under the sink?"

Youngman chuckled. "Negative. Light switch operative. Lab quiet. Everything okay."

"Shut 'er down," the Commander instructed.

The witches waited until he returned to the aft console before becoming visible.

"Witchee! That was a close call!"

"No harm done."

Witchard slid down the curved wall and sat in the sink, holding onto the water injector. Witcheena dog-paddled until she could grasp a handhold set in the wall. Soon her shoes were attached to the floor. She sat down with her back against a counter. "I'm out of breath. I use up lots more energy here than at home."

"Me, too," Witchard flashed so the sound of their voices would not be heard. "I need to recharge my magic, too. Going invisible about wiped me out."

"That's something we should tell the folks back home. And The Supreme. She should warn the old crones to think twice before dashing off on a shuttle mission."

"They shouldn't be allowed on board! The *Sweeper* isn't a shuttle bus." He tried to snap his fingers, and

118

couldn't. "Say, another shuttle lifts off next month. The Supreme should rule that no one can stow away without her permission. That would prevent a stampede."

Witcheena thought he was right. "Cape Canaveral could have more witches brooming around than sea gulls. There's no telling the mischief they would do." After a moment she added, "Witchard, we've got to tell The Supreme to forbid witches from pulling any tricks or interfering in any way with NASA projects, or the workmen, or guards, or flight crews. Did I forget anything? Oh, Witchard, I'm afraid! We've all been raised to make trouble for earthlings. Some of those cranky old witches are bound to cause a bad accident."

Witchard frowned. "Yeah! And it'll be my fault because I started this stowaway business. Think! We've got to figure how to save the shuttle missions from witches. As soon as we slip into the flight deck, I'll call The Supreme on the downlink. If both of us let her know how worried we are, she'll do the right thing."

12
"Don't expect a miracle"

The two sat in the dark so long, thinking hard, that the *Sweeper* completed another of its ninety-minute orbits of the Earth, and sunrise lightened the sky. The blackness bleached to gray, and the gray to sparkling pink and yellow. Swiftly the pale glow of the portion of the planet facing the sun reflected dazzling golden-white light glimpsed through tendrils of rose-tipped clouds.

Witcheena's eyes began to droop, so Witchard magicked her into staying awake. Then he yawned, and she magicked him the same way. Laughing, they agreed to do this whenever one or the other got drowsy, particularly during the hours they hoped to spend in the flight deck.

Due to the speed at which the orbiter traveled, the sunrise lasted only eight seconds and daylight about forty-five minutes. Sunset was very brief.

Anxious to see their planet from space, the two put on sunglasses and stood to look out the window. Both were almost overcome by the beauty of the world glimpsed below. Suddenly the Earth disappeared behind a dense white cloud cover.

"Oh, bats!" Witcheena exclaimed.

"We'll see it lots more times, during other orbits."

She eyed him. "Are you really going to try and contact the Pioneers? Or were you just bragging?"

The question stung. "I wouldn't brag about that. I'm going to try right after I reach Gramwitch and The Supreme. But don't expect a miracle. We're orbiting only 172 miles above the Earth. That's awfully low. The U.S. early warning satellites are in stationary orbit 23,500 miles high. The moon is 238,000 miles away. The nearest galaxy is nearly two million *light years* away. If the Pioneers didn't get any farther out than the moon, we're in luck. If they flew on past into deep space, the chances of our signal reaching them are pretty thin." He asked, "Didn't you realize how far off our folks could be?"

Her chin trembled. "I didn't want to know. Remember how near the stars seem some nights when we're flying around? You think you could almost reach out and touch them? That's the picture I clung to."

"I asked my homeroom teacher, Mr. Abbott, how long it might take a voice transmission from an orbiter flying about 180 miles above the Earth to reach the moon, and then the nearest star, and then the planet Mars. We worked a skillion equations on the blackboard." He murmured, "We didn't come up with very satisfactory answers. Mr. Abbott said that was because there were too many variables."

"You didn't tell him why you wanted an answer."

"Heck, no. If I'd said my parents were buzzing around out there, Mr. Abbott would have sent me to the school counselor."

"Even if it was the truth?"

"How could I prove it was, or wasn't, the truth? When I first started school, I told lots of people I was a witch. They either laughed or said I'd watched *Star Trek* too much."

"How long will it take to send a message out to the Pioneers, and get back an answer?" she asked.

"Minutes. Maybe hours. We've never been successful transmitting from Earth, so nobody knows. It's kind of hard to explain. See, we have to be lined up with the Pioneers almost straight above us before we can reach them and they can answer back. If they're on one side of the Earth and we're on the other, it won't work. Understand?"

Witcheena nodded.

"Then we also have to be on the same witch frequency. There are four we all use, but there could be others we don't know about. So I have to change from one frequency to the other. Every half hour we're in the cockpit, I plan to transmit the same message six times on one frequency, then six on the other three. I'll wait maybe ten minutes between using each frequency."

Witcheena groaned. "I'll go bonkers waiting for an answer. Look, would a message go farther, and be stronger, if we put our hats together to add a double whammy of magic?"

Witchard hadn't planned on sharing his grand experiment with a Junior Witch. He waffled. "Well, let's see if I can reach Gramwitch first. That's the first step. She knows how to use our WF transceiver to tune in on the shuttle. It's no big deal. The directions for Earth ham operators were printed in the newspapers and were on Spacevision. I'm pretty sure I can talk to her because our home WF is as powerful as a 150-watt transmitter. She's going to stay tuned in every night we're up here. Knowing Gram, she's told The Supreme and her cousin Florrie and your aunt to do the same."

Witcheena perked up. "If I talk to Auntie, I'll be

the first Junior Witch to broadcast from an orbit!"

"I'll be the first, witch or wizard. You can't talk until I tune in on Gram."

Witcheena wrinkled her nose at him. "Okay, be first. But how are you going to tune in if you can't touch anything?"

He laughed. "You're asking a witch? With magic!"

He turned around and sat down, clasping his hands under his knees. Witcheena sat facing him. He asked her, "Did you come up with any good ideas?"

"Ideas for what?"

"What to tell The Supreme to keep tricky old crones from wrecking future missions. They're not about to give up their life's work."

Witcheena confessed she had concentrated on what to say to her parents when he contacted the Pioneers. Suddenly she muttered, "All we do is sit around and wait, wait, wait! If I was home, I could climb on Cadenza, and broom off somewhere. I'm going into the airlock and try on a space suit."

"You are not!"

Her eyes glittered. "Why not? There's no space walk scheduled. They aren't going to be used on this mission."

"Because you promised not to touch anything."

"Oh, bats!" After a long pause she snapped, "Aren't those men ever going to bed?"

As if in answer to her complaint, both heard Control announce the crew had permission to "shut 'er down."

They peered through the walls in order to watch what happened. Commander McKenzie inserted a code card into the computer. This switched the *Sweeper* to computerized automatic control. He turned off the speakers and closed-circuit television and removed his headset. Before leaving the flight deck, he put on a battery-powered beeper so he could be wakened in an emergency.

The pilot and specialists followed him to the mid-deck. After personal hygiene, they crawled into their sleep station bunks and zipped up their sleeping bags.

Without asking Witchard's permission, Witcheena magicked all four immediately into deep sleep. Then she clomped straight through the airlock and mid-deck, and climbed to the flight deck. She vaulted into the pilot's seat, pressed her shoes against the floor to secure the microgravity attachments, and snapped the seat belt. Her hat was lopsided, but she didn't care. "Okay, I'm ready. Start transmitting."

Witchard was in a daze. He looked around, his fingers twitching. "I'm here," he murmured. "I made it!" He could not remember ever being so happy.

The sketches he had studied in the shuttle operator's manual had familiarized him with everything on the extremely crowded flight deck. He felt as if he had crawled up inside a pulsing, humming, blinking computer. For a second he closed his eyes to imprint the feeling in his memory.

He was not afraid. He did not feel boxed in.

He felt very much at home.

13
"WCQ, WCQ, WCQ..."

"Are you going to transmit standing up?" Witcheena teased.

Witchard slid onto the flight commander's seat, wrapped his legs around the control stick and engaged the seat belt. "The Supreme told me I could use the pilot's shortwave radio because I'm an experienced operator and wouldn't damage it. It belongs to Pilot Ransome, not NASA, and isn't connected with the orbiter."

He lifted a small lightweight walkie-talkie type ham radio from the front console, and placed it on his lap. "Here's the antenna, or aerial, stitched onto this card. When I'm transmitting, you'll have to hold the card against the window so nothing blocks the transmission or reception of our witch frequencies. When you're transmitting, I'll hold it up there."

"You're not going to use the astronaut's headset?"

"I'd sure like to. I probably could hear better, and

my voice would transmit clearer. But I'm not supposed—"

Witcheena handed him the lightweight headset which
consisted of an earphone and wire-thin microphone.
"Here. Use it! There's no way an experienced operator
like you could hurt it. You should do everything you
can to make contact with the Pioneers possible."

Witchard didn't need much convincing. He put the
headset in place, and clipped its small control unit to
his waistband. One cable connected the headset to the
control unit, and another extending from the bottom
plugged into the set on his lap.

"How will I hear if the Pioneers answer?" Witcheena
asked.

Feeling it was not fair for her to miss out on something as exciting as that, Witchard told her to put on
the other headset and control unit. A magic word made
her apparatus' plug-in fit alongside his. She did so
quickly. "Are we all set?"

"Almost." The control clipped to his waistband was
called the audio terminal unit, he explained. "See, it
has a rocker switch marked Receive and another marked
Transmit. I'll transmit, then—Whoops! I forgot to
change the pilot's set from Earth to witch frequencies."
He muttered several magic words this time, and stamped
both feet. A red light glowed on the set. "Okay, we

got WF. See, the astronauts' signals go on an uplink to a Tracking and Data Relay Satellite high above the Earth. From there the signals are bounced to a ground station—at White Sands, New Mexico, I think—and then on to Houston. NASA keeps improving its communications setup on every mission, so what I said could be out-of-date now."

"It doesn't matter. Will your transmissions to Earth have to go up first to that satellite before they go down to Earth?"

They wouldn't because he would be transmitting on witch frequencies which went up, down, and in all directions.

He looked up at the tip of Witcheena's hat and was relieved to see it did not interfere with the switches over their heads. "Is my pennant flying like yours?" Assured it was, he exclaimed, "Now my words will fly!"

He transmitted in witch language on the WF. "WCQ, WCQ, WCQ (Witch Frequency calling), Breaker Low-Orbit Shuttle. Gram's Imp, number 7068, calling Gramwitch, WF Northwest Sector." He repeated this five times at one-minute intervals, concluding, "Come back. Over."

He and Witcheena held their breaths while waiting to hear an acknowledgment. When none came, he was worried. "Before I left, I gave Gram the approximate time I would be transmitting, and she knows the frequency."

Witcheena whooped. "I forgot to hold the antenna up against the window. Why do I have to stand to do it? Can't I just magic it up there?" Without waiting for his answer, she made the card sail overhead and fasten itself against the window.

"And I forgot to move the rocker switch to Receive in order to hear a call back." He set the switch properly.

"We're doing dumb things because we're so excited. I just had a great idea. When I talk to Auntie, could I ask to hear Angela meow? I miss both dreadfully." She giggled. "That would be the first cat's meow transmitted to space." After a moment she added, "Too bad I didn't bring her along. She's expecting again and might have had her kittens on board! Wouldn't that be something? What would we call them? Spacekits? Astrokittens?"

Witchard motioned for quiet. "It's about time for a call back."

Shortly after, both heard a voice transmitting faintly in their language. "Breaker WF Northwest. Can't copy. Repeat. Can't copy. Come back. Over."

Witchard almost popped his seat belt. "That's Gram. She can't hear my signal clearly. I'll try another frequency." He magicked the radio, repeated his message, adding "All okay here" before concluding, "Come back. Over." Then he remembered to switch over to Receive.

Because the two were used to speedy flash-talk and immediate answers when transmitting on the WF at home, they found waiting two minutes for an answer seemed like hours. However, in time they heard Gramwitch distinctly. "Important visitors here. The Supreme broomed in to share this history-making moment. Scarey and Witcheena's Auntie also here. All thrilled to hear your voice. Do you copy? Over."

Witchard raised his fists in a victory sign. "I want to send another message. Then you can have your turn," he told Witcheena.

He transmitted, "Greetings from *Sweeper*! Advise Supreme hold all space stowaway travel permits until we return. Orbiter extremely crowded. Magic works. Tricking of any kind so dangerous we are not witching anything. Come back. Over."

After switching to Receive again, he confessed, "Now I can relax. I feel like a ten-ton asteroid lifted off my chest. Now maybe the *Challenger* and *Columbia* and any other shuttles won't be overloaded with witch stowaways on their missions."

"But you fibbed! We are too experimenting with little things."

"Yeah, like snitching granola bars."

They received greetings and congratulations from The Supreme. "You have pioneered a new career for our people, Witchard. Now we can have observers on space missions. I expect a written report. Over and out."

Witcheena made a horrible face. "Written report. Yuck!" She placed one hand over her microphone, and whispered, "I just know The Supreme will name a new category after us. We might be called the first space observers, or something like that." She bounced on her seat. "We'll be the most famous witches in all witchdom!"

Witchard puffed out his chest. "Hey, you're right. You acknowledge. Say something fancy to The Supreme."

The Junior Witch moved the rocker switch on her control unit to Transmit, and so did Witchard on his. Then she cleared her throat, identified herself, and said, "We are thrilled to expand the WF network into space. Much to observe here. Beautiful experience. Comfy hiding place." She thanked The Supreme for her kind words. Then she asked politely if she might speak to Auntie and Angela.

Auntie talked a flood until Gramwitch cut her off. Then Angela meowed greetings. Since many witches were eavesdropping on their home WF sets, an enor-

mous flare-up of *dit-dit-dits* filled the airwaves. Crones from coast to coast cackled gleefully.

The *Sweeper* completed two more orbits before Witchard signed off. He and Witcheena had received many greetings from OAW members. Sometimes they heard as many as four voices at the same time, all demanding answers. Were the astronauts good looking? What magic did the scientists use in the laboratory? Several suggested very dangerous tricks.

Witchard and Witcheena tried not to offend any Senior Witches. At the same time they said over and over that witches should never play tricks on a shuttle mission because it was extremely dangerous. They said they had promised The Supreme not to touch anything for fear of destroying the mission.

Witchard transmitted, "Witch tricks have no place on any space mission. We're not playing space war games. We're serious! We're here to try and contact our Pioneers, and maybe bring them back. Anything that hurts the *Sweeper* or its crew hurts us. So pipe down, you cranky old tricksters! Get off the air so we can get on with our search-and-rescue broadcasts. We will report same time tomorrow night, same frequency. Over and out."

He was so disgusted with the old crones' suggestions that he turned off the set for a few moments. "There! That ought to fix them."

Witcheena was very upset. "You're not allowed to sass your elders. When you get home, someone might turn you into a toad."

"No one would dare. The Supreme and Gram will protect both of us, and the space shuttle." He pressed back against the headrest and closed his eyes. "I'm going to rest a little before I transmit to outer space."

Too upset and nervous to sit still, Witcheena unbuckled and headed for the ladder. "I'm going to clean up and comb my hair."

Witchard was glad to be alone. He had some heavy thinking to do. Transmitting far into space was not as simple as talking to Gram. The big problem was he did not know where the Pioneers were. Were they directly above the *Sweeper*, or off to the side enough to make contact impossible, or maybe over on the opposite side of the Earth? With the *Sweeper* speeding at 17,500 miles per hour in orbit, its position changed constantly. Fortunately, WF frequencies were very strong. When amateur radio operators on Earth had contacted the astronaut who was the first to bring his ham radio set on board, they had to time their transmissions into a known time period. They were successful because they had figured the exact period when the shuttle would be within range over the United States. He didn't have that kind of help. There was no exact time to contact the Pioneers because repeated transmissions on the WF on the times they had agreed on had produced no messages. Something must have altered the Pioneers' position, and therefore the time they could be reached.

The chances of his transmissin hitting its target were slim, but Witchard would not let that keep him from trying hour after hour.

When he turned on the amateur shortwave radio again, he was surprised to see Witcheena back in her seat. "I'm going to transmit the same message on even minutes—at two, four, and six minutes past the hour—and leave the WF on uneven minutes so the Pioneers can answer without interference from us. I'll also transmit on our four witch frequencies each hour. If that doesn't cover outer space, nothing will!"

"You're going to transmit from now until we go to sleep?"

"Have to," he answered. "I'll need you to spell me off."

"You know I'll do my best."

"Okay, we're coming up on two minutes past the hour. Here goes." He transmitted slowly and clearly, "WCQ, WCQ, WCQ, Breaker Low-Orbit Shuttle. Gram's Imp, number 7068, calling Pioneers Dearie and Darrell. Wake up. Repeat wake up. Important message. Advise location. Call back. Over."

After three repetitions, he told Witcheena, "Be sure and use your parents' names. My folks might be in a deep trance and not hear the signal. But Gram told me long ago there always would be two Pioneers awake and acting as navigators and message transmitters. Someone should hear us, I hope."

The two grimly stayed with transmitting, repeating and listening for signals until time to leave the cockpit. They weren't too disappointed at hearing no response because both knew of the enormous distance involved, and the elusive period when the Pioneers might hear them.

"We'll try again tomorrow night," he said as he placed the headsets in their proper holders, turned off the set, and magicked it back to its former state.

The next evening his first transmission was to Gramwitch. But Scarey's voice was heard instead. "Gramwitch too exhausted to talk. The Supreme postponed all space travel permits. Hundreds are waiting to contact you two. Call them by name. They want to hear their names broadcast from the shuttle. Don't disappoint them. Bye-bye. Love you both. Over and out."

Immediately a torrent of questions filled the cockpit. Witchard turned off the radio, only to have Witcheena turn it back on. She warned, "Do what Scarey said. You can't disappoint the callers. Some would get mad, and make trouble." She transmitted until Witchard got his temper under control.

Six hours passed in answering questions. Although Witchard begged callers to leave the air so he could transmit and also search for calls from outer space, the witches ignored him.

Exhausted and hoarse, he dispatched a distress signal to Supreme headquarters. Immediately all chatter ceased. The Supreme responded, much to his relief. He begged frantically, "Please make OAW members withhold all calls tomorrow night so we can try to contact the Pioneers. We have been flooded with so many calls tonight that we can't do anything but repeat their names over the air." He was so tired and desperate he cried out, "If those witches don't shut up, we'll never contact our parents!"

The Supreme issued a stern command for all OAW members to stay off the air, or face expulsion. Then she said, "Young witches, report your progress every twenty-four hours at this time. I will monitor WF personally. OAW extremely proud of you two. Inviting you to present full report at national convention in March. Over and out."

Witchard turned off the set and whispered to Witcheena because it was near time for the flight crew to waken. "Did you hear that? We're to address the national convention!"

"We'll be the first Junior Witches ever to do that," she flash-answered. "Witchee!"

He winced. "You darn near split my eardrums. Let's call it quits. I'm falling asleep."

The two unbuckled and stumbled their way to bed.

14

"Let's fib a little"

When the two took their places in the cockpit the next evening, Witchard asked, "Ready for another workout, pal?"

Witcheena shook her hat. "Not quite. I have an idea. Instead of asking the Pioneers to call back, why don't we fib a little? We might have only one chance, so why not say something they have to acknowledge?"

"Like what?"

She rolled her eyes. "Well, what about saying 'Supreme urges your immediate return.' Or, if that isn't strong enough, add 'Families need you.' That ought to get some reaction."

Witchard liked her idea but felt he must protest. "The Supreme didn't tell us to say that."

"She wouldn't get mad if they did come back. If the Pioneers hear that The Supreme commands them to come home, they'll turn around and start back right away. I know they might not hear us, but isn't it worth a try?"

Witchard responded excitedly, "I'll do it! Neither of us wants to live in space, so why should our folks stay out there looking for a new planet? All their families miss them. Maybe they want to come home, but won't unless The Supreme tells them to. Yes, let's fib a little."

After transmitting four messages imploring the Pioneers to wake up and follow The Supreme's command to return home immediately, they leaned back and talked quietly. Witchard said, "Last night you said one space trip was enough for you. Wouldn't you go again if you had the chance?"

Witcheena shook her hat slowly. "I'd need an awfully good reason. I like being a Resident Witch. I want to live on Earth, and be an animal doctor later on."

"I plan to be an astronaut," Witchard vowed. "But I couldn't spend months, or years, in a permanent space station. I'd miss school, and my pals, and soccer games. And Halloween! What would witches do if they moved to a treeless planet where there weren't any other people? They'd have only themselves to haunt and scare.

"In my part of our report, I'm going to dare to say that witches should stop thinking about leaving Earth for a faraway planet. And another thing, they should stop haunt-and-scare tricks. They were okay in the olden days, but not in the space age."

Witcheena pointed out that if witches and wizards didn't have something to do, they'd cause all sorts of mischief.

"Then let them work toward making the Earth a better place to live. Lots of earthlings are doing it. Why shouldn't we? Haunt-and-scare tricks are a terrible waste of magic. We should spy on polluters. If we caught them dumping waste, we could throw it back in their faces! We could expose timber thieves, and marijuana growers, and towns which dump raw sewage into rivers, and big oil spills . . . lots of things.

"But my big dream is to have my folks come back so we can be together."

Witcheena had nodded so many times her hat fell off. She put it back on. "The trouble is, we can write or talk our heads off, and only a few Senior Witches will listen to us. They don't think we have anything important to say."

"The Supreme listened to me. And Scarey. She made Gram back off from forcing me to stay home. Scarey may sound like a scaredy-cat, but she'll back us 100 percent."

"So will Auntie. Oh, Witchard, if you get word to the Pioneers to come home, every family in the OAW will love you." She smiled. "You know what? You're a genius. You're the smartest wizard in the world." Then she teased, "What makes you so fabulous?"

Witchard blushed so much his cheeks glowed in the dark. "Oh, it's not hard when you have lots of help."

"I haven't done very much."

"I'll level with you. I wanted to make this trip alone. I wanted it to be all mine from start to finish. I didn't ask Scarey to go with me. Gram made her. I was thrilled when she chickened out. Then you took her place. I didn't like that at all. I was sure you'd be bossy, and talk all the time, and crack your gum like the girls in my class. But I was wrong. You've been a really good sport. You're as good a pal as Ted, my school chum. I never thought a Junior Witch could be a real pal, but you sure are."

Witcheena's eyes glowed, and gave off twinkling golden sparks. "Now I'll level with you. I've always hated Junior Wizards. They're the bossy ones, and so conceited! But I'd be thrilled to have you for a special friend."

Witchard extended his hand. "Let's shake on that."

Suddenly shy, the two remained silent until time to move to the flight deck. They had to wait longer than the previous nights because Pilot Ransome transmitted to ham radio operators in the United States. They jammed the airwaves with their calls back as the *Sweeper*

143

sped high above from the west coast to the east coast. Witcheena waited until the pilot crawled into his bunk before magicking all the crew into a deep sleep. Then she and Witchard climbed up into the flight deck.

The two devoted the entire night and early morning hours to transmitting to the Pioneers, and listening for any kind of response, strong or weak, by voice or the witch version of the Morse code. Thanks to the stern command issued by The Supreme, they encountered no interference from witches on Earth.

By midnight their bodies ached from built-up tension. Each relaxed by walking a few steps, or gazing below at their beautiful homeland during the brief glowing sunrises and sunsets. About 3:00 A.M. Witcheena climbed down to the mid-deck. She returned with hot coffee and a pack of chocolate chip cookies.

Just before 6:00 A.M. Witchard transmitted to The Supreme, "No luck so far. Will try again tomorrow night."

Early on their fourth and last visit to the cockpit before the *Sweeper* headed home, Witcheena struggled to be cheerful. As hours passed without the slightest response from the Pioneers, she became very upset. "We're never going to hear from them!"

"Hang tough," Witchard urged. But by 4:00 A.M. he, too, had almost given up hope. "We still have an hour

144

or maybe a little more to transmit before I sign off. Tomorrow night the crew stays in the cockpit to get the *Sweeper* ready for the return home." He pounded his knees. "Oh, witchit! All those calls, and no answers. We'll never know if the Pioneers heard us."

"I don't think I can stand to talk any more," Witcheena remarked. "Let's just listen."

With their rocker switches set on Receive, they heard the familiar crackling static. But soon a different far-away sound drew their attention.

"Did you hear something?"

Witcheena gulped. "I think so."

"Shhh!"

"You shhh!"

In vain they strained to hear better.

Witcheena remembered that if they put their hat tips together, they would have increased hearing ability.

Immediately after the tips were joined, both heard, "WCQ, WCQ, WCQ, WCQ . . . Pioneers Expedition calling orbiting *Sweeper*. Advise your messages received. Advise Supreme Pioneers will head home immediately. Over. Out."

Witcheena opened her mouth to squeal, but Witchard clamped his hand over it. The message was repeated, and then the voice faded out. The two hugged

each other, waiting for another repeat. There was none.

"Did you recognize the voice? Was it your father?" Witcheena asked.

"No. I didn't recognize it. D'you think it was your father?"

"I could barely hear over the static. No, I'm sure it wasn't Darrell."

"Got to call The Supreme," Witchard said, pushing the switch to Transmit. As soon as she acknowledged, he exclaimed, "We got it, we got it, we just heard someone from the Pioneers! He said, 'Advise Supreme Pioneers heading home.' Then he repeated so we heard him a second time. We had to put our hat tips together to hear, and even then it was hard. After that whoever it was . . . he didn't give his name . . . must have stopped transmitting because we heard nothing more."

Witcheena interrupted. "We're not fibbing. We're not pulling a trick. We really did hear every word."

"Stand by while I make an official announcement of your marvelous news!"

Keeping their audio unit on Receive, the overjoyed juniors heard The Supreme transmit, "Attention! This is The Supreme speaking. Clear airwaves for exciting news from the orbiter."

After waiting five seconds for WF operators to stop talking, she continued, "Witchard and Witcheena have just confirmed contact with our Pioneers. Unidentified member reports they are coming home." She repeated the glorious news, and then advised all to stand by for another announcement.

"Witchard and Witcheena, your courageous accomplishment has inspired me to create a new category in witchdom, that of Astrowitch.

"I hereby name you both to equal rank as First Astrowitches of the Organization of American Witches.

"My staff will arrange a gala homecoming in your

honor as soon as we know the landing site. Weather over Florida poor so it may be at Edwards Air Force Base. All OAW members urged to be present. Tune in tomorrow for instructions and directions. The Cabinet and I will attend. Over. Out."

Although churning with excitement, Witchard had presence of mind to transmit a warning to The Supreme. "Advise strict air traffic control at reception area, wherever it is. Helicopters clear flight path two hours before touchdown. Military planes escort *Sweeper* to wheels stop. Witcheena and I appreciate great honor bestowed on us! Glad our mission goal accomplished. Witchee! Over and out!"

15

A Gala Homecoming

After a comfortable day's sleep in their lockers, Witchard and Witcheena wakened to the familiar sounds of the crew's conversation while eating dinner. The men were in good spirits and eager to experience re-entering the Earth's atmosphere. Ground Control had alerted them that weather conditions over Cape Canaveral had worsened, so they would land at Edwards Air Force Base in the California desert where the weather was perfect. Except for this change, the most critical part of the mission would proceed as scheduled.

While consuming their Day 5 dinner dessert, lemon pudding and pecan cookies, Control was heard on the intercom, "Time to put on the anti-gravity suits." The latter prevented blackouts during re-entry.

Witcheena flashed worriedly, "We don't have anti-g suits."

"No problem," he flashed back. After they were

149

seated on the mid-deck seats and zipped up inside the rescue bags again, they would magic themselves into a trance. "Our bodies will remain stable while we're zooming down through the Earth's atmosphere, and then automatically return to normal as we glide down to twenty thousand feet. Just remember to turn on your oxygen tank before you put yourself to sleep."

As soon as the mission scientists pulled on their anti-gravity suits, they checked the laboratory to make certain everything was in proper order for deorbit. Dr. Browne placed the rats' cage inside its rescue bag, turned on the oxygen, and zipped it shut. He closed the airlock hatches firmly. Next the two secured the hygiene station, galley, bunks, and all storage lockers.

Watching all this from inside his hiding place, Witchard grinned when Dr. Browne took extra pains bracing the two mid-deck seats in their storage area.

The mechanical arm and grinder in the cargo bay had been secured, and the huge doors closed. The scientists pulled out their seats, stowed during orbit, and buckled up. The crew was ready when Control announced, "*Sweeper*, you are Go for deorbit."

Witchard broke out in goose pimples from head to toe. "Witchee, we're really heading home! Come on," he flashed to Witcheena. "Time to move out!"

Speedily he used magic to flip open the latches on their hiding places, raise the doors, and then move their seats out of their storage area. They locked the seats into travel mode, and got into the rescue bags Witcheena had retrieved and opened. Both sat down, fastened leg and waist belts, arranged the oxygen tanks and face masks properly, and magicked their hats small enough to tuck inside the cover. When they had zipped the long zippers, Witchard flashed, "Don't worry about not having enough power to go into a deep trance. We only need to be out of touch about twelve to fifteen minutes."

As soon as he was comfortable and had his fingers on the oxygen valve, Witchard returned to listening and watching the activity in the cockpit.

Colonel McKenzie and Pilot Ransome were going through the precise maneuvers to get the shuttle out of orbit and back into the Earth's atmosphere and ready for landing. When Ground Control stated that they had Landing minus one hour, the orbiter was turned around until it flew tail-first, to reduce speed. Then engines were ignited for the deorbit burn. When speed had been reduced by 200 miles per hour, the orbiter was turned around again and its nose pointed up slightly higher than before.

Witchard's heart leaped when he heard the Colonel report, "Control, we are in entry attitude at Landing minus fifty-two minutes. Over." Control confirmed this was correct.

The Commander and Pilot busied themselves with preparing the hydraulic systems for landing and dumped remaining propellants in the forward reaction control system. At $L-0:35:00$ the crew inflated their anti-gravity suits.

Witchard flashed to Witcheena, "Turn on your oxygen now and go into a trance."

They regained consciousness in time to hear Colonel McKenzie report to Control, "Everything looking good."

"You all right? Can you hear okay?" Witchard flashed.

Witcheena flashed a bit fuzzily, "I'm fine."

When they heard the Commander state that *Sweeper* had completed its second S-turn in the series of maneuvers to lose more altitude and speed, Witchard flashed exictedly, "Try to look out the window. Oh, witchit, you can't see anything. We're flying right side up now. I was hoping we could see the runway."

"This far up?"

Three minutes before landing, the orbiter was at 50,000 feet. "We're getting closer!" Witchard flashed.

One minute later Control instructed, "Begin auto-land guidance."

"That means landing with instrument assistance," Witchard informed Witcheena. "Can you see the computer display screen? It shows the descent trajectory."

Witcheena took a quick glance, and felt better. The

screen displayed the path the pilot was to follow so clearly that she just knew the landing would be a good one. She strained to hear every word coming through the intercom on the mid-deck.

At Landing minus thirty seconds the Commander stated, "Altitude 2,000 feet, 350 miles per hour. Beginning preflare . . ." Seconds later it was, "Deploying landing gear . . ."

Control's voice barked, "Gear down. Over."

"Roger. Gear down and locked . . . speed brake to 100 percent . . . main gear at ten feet . . . five feet . . . two feet . . . one . . . contact. Touchdown!"

Witchard flashed, "Witchee! We're home safe!"

Witcheena replied, "I knew we'd make it!"

Control shouted joyfully, "*Sweeper*, welcome home!"

The crew remained seated until the pilot turned off the power units and control systems. Then they deflated their anti-g suits, unplugged their life-support systems, and released their seat belts. They rose, shouting and pounding each other exuberantly.

Witchard and Witcheena unzipped hurriedly and magicked the seats and rescue bags out of sight. A few finger flicks and magic routines produced their brooms and uniforms and slickers out from under the mattresses in the bunks. Witcheena kissed Cadenza and then slipped on Scarey's black slicker. Witchard hugged

Splinters and donned his green slicker. Both rolled their uniforms tighter and slipped them into the roomy slicker pockets.

Witcheena tried to jump up and down, but seemed glued to the floor. She giggled, and stripped off her microgravity shoe straps. "Witchee! No more weightlessness! Hurry and open the hatch so we can get out of here!"

Witchard couldn't do that. "It won't unlock until a crew has cleaned the air with blowers, and used air scrubbers on the exterior. We're going to have to hide until the crew leaves. We'll wait until they are hurrying down the steps and we have space to ourselves. Then swoosh out the hatch."

Witcheena made a face, but tucked herself back into her hiding place.

Thirty minutes passed before a spotlight focused on the outside of the hatch, and Commander McKenzie opened it. He stepped out, smiling and waving. Pilot Ransome followed, and then the two mission specialists.

Witchard flashed, "Go invisible. Locker doors up. Brooms, lift off!"

The two jumped to the floor lightly, mounted their brooms and streaked out of the orbiter. The First Astrowitches in witchdom soared to meet their honor guard, circling invisibly above but signaling so Witchard and Witcheena could locate them.

Both squealed joyfully when they heard the voices of Gramwitch, Scarey, and Auntie. "Follow us to the Welcome Home Party out on the desert!"

They responded, "Roger! Over and out!"

MARIAN T. PLACE is the author of over forty books for young people. She is the recipient of four Golden Spur Awards given by the Western Writers of America for Best Western juvenile novel and Best Western juvenile nonfiction title. She won the 1977 Garden State Children's Book Award for *On the Track of Bigfoot* and the 1982 Mark Twain Award for *The Boy Who Saw Bigfoot*.

Marian Place has worked as a newspaperwoman and a children's librarian. She and her husband live in Arizona. They have viewed the space launch facilities at Cape Canaveral, and spent four days observing preparations for the landing of the STS-9 *Columbia* at Edwards AFB in California.

Readers who met Witchard in *The Witch Who Saved Halloween* and Witcheena in *The Resident Witch* by Marian Place will be delighted with the antics of the two in space. Suspense and danger build as they manage to get aboard, accomplish their goal, and not be discovered.

TOM O'SULLIVAN has illustrated forty-eight children's books, as well as textbooks, adult titles, and for national magazines. Born in Brooklyn, he studied sculpture and painting in a WPA Art Project and at the Art Students League, then taught at the School of Visual Arts. While in the Coast Guard, he served as combat artist. He lives in New York City.